NEWS FOR DOGS

ALSO BY LOIS DUNCAN

NEWS FOR DOGS

BY LOIS DUNCAN

Scholastic Inc.

NEW YORK TORONTO LONDON AUCKLAND SYDNEY
MEXICO CITY NEW DELHI HONG KONG BUENOS AIRES

ISBN-13: 978-0-545-10853-9
ISBN-10: 0-545-10853-5

Copyright © 2009 by Lois Duncan

All rights reserved. Published by Scholastic Inc.,
Publishers since 1920. SCHOLASTIC and
associated logos are trademarks and/or registered trademarks
of Scholastic Inc.

12 11 10 9 8 7 6 5 4 3 2 1   9 10 11 12 13 14/0

Printed in the U.S.A.
First printing, April 2009

Book design by Tim Hall

For my three youngest grandchildren,
Holly, Brandon, and Nicholas Arquette,
with love

CHAPTER ONE

"I think we should start a newspaper for dogs," Andi said.

"You think — *what*?" Bruce Walker regarded his sister with astonishment. He had arrived home from school to find her sitting on the front steps waiting for him with her two dogs, Bebe and Friday, on either side of her. They looked like mismatched bookends, as Friday was a shaggy white hairball and Bebe, a dachshund, looked more like a sausage.

Elmwood Elementary let out an hour before the middle school, so Andi always beat Bruce home, but she didn't usually wait outside to intercept him. She did that only when she had something important to tell him or when, like today, she'd come up with some outrageous project.

"I think we should start a newspaper," Andi repeated. "There's nothing for people to read to their dogs these days. Dogs need their own news-paper with articles written just for them."

"That's the dumbest thing I ever heard," Bruce said. "Even if dogs liked the stories, they couldn't buy newspapers, because they don't have money. Please, move so I can get into the house. I want to get something to eat before I take Red for his run."

Andi got up and, with a dog tucked under each arm, trailed him into the house.

"Where's Mom?" Bruce asked. Back when they lived in New Mexico, Mrs. Walker had been a teacher, but she hadn't yet found a teaching posi-tion in Elmwood, so, temporarily at least, she was a stay-at-home mother.

"She and Aunt Alice went to the mall," Andi said. She set the dogs on the floor and watched with a fond expression as they raced hopefully to their food bowls. "Whatever you're going to fix, I'll have some, too. And so will Bebe and Friday."

"You can make your own sandwich," Bruce said, taking a loaf of bread from the cupboard and rum-maging around for the peanut butter. "And those dogs shouldn't snack between meals. They're fat enough already." It was all he could do not to add, "and so are you," but he managed to stop himself from saying it. Andi was a little too chubby, but not exactly fat, and Bruce, although almost always truthful, was seldom unkind.

So, even though he had told her that he wouldn't make her a sandwich, he made one anyway and then watched with dismay as she tore off the crust and dropped a piece into each of the dog bowls. Bebe and Friday gobbled them up so quickly that they almost choked.

"See how hungry they were?" Andi said. "You may like your dog to be bony, but I want mine to be comfortable. I also want my dogs to have cultural experiences."

Bruce poured a glass of milk to wash down his sandwich and took a biscuit for Red Rover out of a tin on the "dog food shelf." There were lots of cans on that shelf, and Bruce had bought most of them himself. That was part of the agreement he had made with his parents when they reluctantly allowed him to own an Irish setter.

"It will be like feeding a horse," his father had commented, which turned out to be true. Although Red was lean and fit, he did eat a lot.

Mr. and Mrs. Walker had never expected to have a three-dog family. They had given Bebe to Andi the same Christmas that they had given Bruce his first camera, but the other dogs had popped into their lives unexpectedly. Friday had turned up on their doorstep during a rainstorm, and Andi had found Red Rover, severely injured, huddling in Aunt Alice's backyard. Red had belonged to Jerry Gordon, who lived next door to Aunt Alice, but when Jerry's father was forced to realize how badly Jerry was mistreating the dog, he had agreed to sell Red to Bruce.

Now, as they sat at the kitchen table eating their sandwiches, Andi continued to chatter about her new grand plan.

"Of course, dogs won't buy the papers. Their owners will do that. Babies can't buy things either, but there are lots of books for babies. Parents buy them and read them to their children. That's how it will be with our newspaper."

"Don't call it *our* newspaper," Bruce said. "This is your idea. If you want to waste your time writing stories for dogs, then go for it. You're the writer in the family. You don't need me."

"But I do!" Andi exclaimed. "I need you to be my photographer and take pictures of things that dogs would be interested in."

"Like cats?" Bruce suggested, trying to conceal his amusement.

"That's one possibility," Andi said solemnly. "An occasional cat would be all right, especially if a dog was chasing it. But, in general, I think dogs would prefer to read about each other. We'll have feature stories about dogs doing feats of bravery, and a gossip column for dogs, and articles about things that dogs can do to have fun."

"And a nutrition column about how bread crusts make dogs fat?"

Bruce placed his glass in the dishwasher. He had hoped his final comment would end the conversation, but when he turned to go out the kitchen door, Andi was right behind him. When his sister got an idea in her head she never let go.

As they stepped out into the yard, Red Rover came bounding to meet Bruce as if he had been counting the minutes until his owner got there. Or his "almost owner." Bruce was saving up to buy Red, but since Irish setters were terribly expensive, it was taking him longer than he'd expected. He had hoped that he could earn money shoveling snow, but there hadn't been any major snowstorms the past winter. Now they were well into spring, and that opportunity was gone. It seemed as if he was destined to go without an earned income until midsummer, when people would need their lawns mowed.

"You know you need money," Andi said as if reading his mind. "We could earn a lot with a newspaper. There are so many dogs in this neighborhood, we'd have a huge readership."

"You're a nut," Bruce said. "Come on, Red, let's go!"

He handed the dog his biscuit as he hooked Red's leash to his collar and looped the strap over his own wrist. When Bruce opened the gate, the big dog plunged through the opening with so much enthusiasm that he almost yanked Bruce off his feet.

Bruce broke into a run to keep up as Red galloped along the sidewalk, his glossy coat shining in the sunlight and his plumed tail waving like a banner. He was the most beautiful animal Bruce had ever seen and was so filled with life and vitality that neighbors, out in their yards preparing their flower beds, broke into smiles to see the two of them run by. It was almost impossible to believe that only six months ago, Red had almost strangled to death when Jerry Gordon had harnessed him to a coaster wagon.

It was Andi who had helped Bruce nurse him back to health. Even though there were times when she drove him crazy, Bruce had to admit that she was a pretty good sister.

I shouldn't have put her down like that, he thought guiltily. *She was so excited about the idea of a dog newspaper. And, dumb as it sounds, there might actually be people who would buy it, if only because an eleven-year-old was the editor.*

Andi was a good writer, he had to give her that. Ever since she was little she had been writing poetry, and she'd started submitting poems to magazines when she was ten. So far she had made no sales, but her poems were published regularly in the school newspaper.

She probably could write articles, Bruce acknowledged. But he didn't know what she'd find to put in them. A gossip column for dogs was really stretching it.

Bruce was so engrossed in his thoughts and in the challenge of keeping up with Red Rover that he wasn't really noticing where they were going until he glanced ahead and saw that they were approaching the intersection where Jerry had caused Red to almost be hit by a car. Ever since then, that intersection had given Bruce chills, and he avoided it if at all possible.

We won't cross that street, he told himself. *Instead, we'll circle the block and head back home.*

He began to rein in Red as they approached the corner. When he heard the whir of wheels behind them and recognized the sound of a skateboard, he moved to the edge of the sidewalk and pulled Red over to permit the skateboarder to pass.

But the skateboarder *didn't* pass. He remained behind them, slowing as if deliberately keeping pace with them.

That's odd, Bruce thought. *Why doesn't he swerve around us?*

He wanted to turn his head to see who was following them, but was worried that he might stumble, so he just kept running and listening to those wheels. Then he felt the front edge of the skateboard nudge the back of his left leg. First it was just a little bump, as if it were an accident, and then enough of a thump so it really hurt.

"Hey, knock it off!" Bruce yelled over his shoulder. "There's plenty of room for you to pass us!"

The skateboard hit him again. This time it struck the calf of his right leg with so much force that he almost tripped. Bruce jumped over onto the lawn of the house to his left. It was obvious now that the idiot behind him was not just a klutz, he was actually launching an attack.

"Whoa, Red!" Bruce shouted as the leash went taut between them.

"*Whoa, Red!*" yelled another voice, echoing his tone so exactly that it was clear that the person behind him was making fun of him. Bruce felt his stomach clench, because this was a voice he recognized and, to his ears, it was the nastiest voice in the world.

"What do you think you're doing, Jerry?" Bruce demanded. "If you don't know how to steer that thing, go home and skate in your driveway!"

He wasn't exactly afraid of Jerry Gordon, but he didn't like the thought of getting into a fight with him. Actually, Bruce didn't like the idea of fighting *anybody*. He was small for his age and not built for physical combat, but it wasn't just his size that made him a peace lover. Bruce was a friendly boy, who genuinely liked people, and most people liked him back. But Jerry had hated Bruce from the first time they met, when Bruce had petted Red Rover without asking Jerry's permission. And Jerry was the sort of enemy who could make your life miserable.

The worst thing of all about Jerry, other than his being cruel and vicious and selfish and spoiled rotten, was that he was able to make grown-ups think he was adorable. He was blond and good-looking and could switch on a sweet fake smile that lit up his face like sunshine. When the Walkers had first come to Elmwood, his father's aunt Alice had beamed as she told them, "That dear boy, Jerry, has a smile that just melts your heart!"

But now, when there weren't any adults around to impress, Jerry's expression was more of a sneer.

"What do we have here?" he exclaimed. "I do believe it's the shrimpy little dog-stealer! I hope you know I'm going to get Red Rover back from you."

"I don't see that happening," Bruce said, trying to sound sure of himself. "Your dad told me I could buy him. He said you weren't ready for the responsibility of a dog."

"People change their minds," Jerry said. "My dad will change his. He was mad at me for a while, but I'm winning him over. That dog is mine, and nobody takes my stuff. Look how he's shaking! He knows the voice of his master!"

Bruce glanced over at Red Rover, who had started to tremble. All the joy of their lovely run seemed to have left him.

"Get over here, Red!" Jerry commanded. "I'm taking you home with me!"

Red looked pleadingly at Bruce and began to whimper. He lowered his head and tucked his bright tail between his legs.

"Don't let him scare you, old boy," Bruce said soothingly. "Jerry is full of hot air."

"That's what you think!" Jerry shouted. He shoved his foot hard against the sidewalk and shot past Bruce on the skateboard, aiming straight for Red Rover.

The dog didn't wait to be hit before reacting.

With a yelp of terror, Red leapt forward so fast that the leash jerked free from Bruce's wrist and his dog plunged off the curb into oncoming traffic.

CHAPTER TWO

There was a blare of horns, a terrible screech of brakes, and shouts of fury from drivers who were swerving all over the road in their frantic efforts to avoid hitting the terrified dog.

"Red!" Bruce shouted. "Get back here!"

It was like reliving a nightmare. Six months ago, when Jerry had hitched Red to a coaster wagon, that wagon had rammed Red's hind legs and sent him plunging out into the middle of this very street. A car had crushed the wagon as Red tore free of the wreckage and kept on running. Now the same thing was happening again, but this time there was no wagon, just a terror-stricken animal trying to dodge the wheels and fenders of a stream of cars.

"Red!" Bruce shouted again and, without pausing to consider his own safety, raced into the street. This caused even more commotion, as the drivers were now forced to dodge a boy as well as a dog. A Ford braked so suddenly that the Chevrolet behind it crashed into its rear fender, causing the Ford to leap the curb and end up with both front wheels on the sidewalk.

By now, the horns and the shouts had brought Red Rover to a standstill. His legs seemed to go out from under him, and he sank down onto the street in a quivering heap. It was only when he saw Bruce running toward him, weaving his way through the pileup of halted vehicles, that he was able to stagger to his feet and hurl himself gratefully into the arms of the person he loved best in the world.

Two of the drivers had gotten out of their cars and were headed in Bruce's direction with grim expressions on their faces. The first was the driver of the Ford. He was followed closely by the driver of the Chevrolet that had hit him. Bruce, who was kneeling in the street with his arms around Red Rover, now could see that the second car had sustained damage also.

"It wasn't my fault!" the driver of the second car yelled at the driver of the first car. "You slammed on your brakes without signaling!"

"You would have been able to stop if you hadn't

been tailgating," the first driver shouted. "The dog and the kid ran straight out in front of me! What did you expect me to do, run over them?"

"Is this your dog?" the second driver demanded of Bruce.

"Yes," Bruce said, but all of his attention was on Red Rover. He gathered the big dog close and spoke to him soothingly. "Are you okay, fella?"

"That is *not* his dog!" Jerry Gordon called out from the sidewalk. The skateboard had mysteriously vanished, and Jerry appeared to be nothing more than a bystander, out for an innocent stroll. His voice was no longer mean as it had been moments earlier. It had changed completely and now was trembling with indignation.

"Red Rover is mine!" Jerry cried. "That kid stole him from me!"

"He *stole* that dog?" exclaimed the motorist whose car was on the sidewalk. "Then it's little wonder the poor animal was trying to escape!" He turned to Bruce. "I want your name and address and the names of your parents."

"So do I!" cried the man who had rear-ended him. "The damage doesn't appear major enough to get the police involved, but we need to sort this out so we can deal with our insurance companies." He went back to his car and returned with paper and a pencil. "I want contact information for your parents," he said to Bruce. He turned to Jerry. "I'd like contact information for you too, son," he said in a gentler voice. "You were a witness to what happened, as well as the person from whom this boy stole the setter. Now that I've had a close look at him, I'm sure he's bred to be a show dog. I certainly hope you reported the theft to the authorities."

"I just want my dog back!" Jerry said in a quavering voice that ended in a sob. His artificial crying was so perfect that, if Bruce hadn't known better, he might have bought it. Jerry was actually squeezing his lids down over his eyes so hard that he was making real tears come out. Bruce wondered how anybody could do that.

"Red doesn't belong to Jerry," he told the two men. "There was a time when he did, but not anymore. Red Rover is mine — or, he will be, when I've finished paying for him."

"Then why don't you take better care of him?" the second driver bellowed while the first driver shook his head in disbelief. "You lost control of this dog and allowed him to run into traffic. And it could have been worse than that! You were very, very lucky. You also ran out into traffic, and one of us could have hit you!"

"I had to save Red!" Bruce's own tears were close to the surface, but he was determined not to let anyone see that. He would not lower himself to behaving like Jerry. Two women, who had been passengers in the cars, had now gotten out to join their husbands and were gathered around Jerry, soothing and comforting him.

"You poor boy!" exclaimed the sweet-faced wife of the driver of the first car. Tears of sympathy were streaming down her own cheeks as she gently stroked Jerry's hair. "Just as you were trying to reclaim your long-lost puppy dog, you almost lost him again — *under the wheels of our car*!"

"That's not how it happened —" Bruce began, but he let the protest fade off when he realized that no one was listening.

After a second round of questioning and rechecking names and phone numbers, the driver of the Ford carefully backed his car off the sidewalk and it landed in the street with a thump. It appeared to be running fine despite a dent in one of the rear fenders. By the time both drivers finally departed, Bruce was so filled with fury that he felt like he was going to explode.

"What did you do with your skateboard?" he demanded of Jerry. "How did you get rid of it so fast?"

"It's over there under those bushes," Jerry said with a grin.

"I might have known that you'd already picked out a hiding place," Bruce said.

"I always know what I'm doing, shrimp," Jerry told him. "I wouldn't want to be you when those guys call your dad. I bet they're going to sue you. But even if they don't, Red Rover's history. I'm going to get him back, and my cousin's going to help me."

"You don't have a cousin," Bruce said. "If you did, I'd have heard of him."

"He's not from around here," Jerry said. "Connor lives in Chicago, but he and I are buddies. We e-mail all the time, and he knows all about you. He's coming to spend the summer as soon as school lets out, and you'd better watch out when he gets here. Nobody messes with Connor. My enemies are *his* enemies."

"Oh, I'm so scared!" Bruce said sarcastically. "Big, bad Connor! Come on, Red, you and I are out of here."

He strode off with his back held straight and his shoulders squared in a way that he hoped might add an inch to his height. He gripped Red's leash as tightly as possible, making sure that the dog was positioned directly in front of him so there was no way that Jerry could get at him. The whir of the wheels of Jerry's skateboard on the sidewalk behind them was a threatening noise that followed them all the way home.

Bruce didn't put Red in the backyard as he usually did after a run. Instead, he took him in through the front door and up the stairs to his own bedroom. Once they were safely inside, he shut the door, sat down on his bed, and patted the mattress beside him. Red gazed up at him in astonishment. He knew that he was not allowed on the furniture.

Bruce patted the mattress again.

"Hop up, boy," he said.

He had already broken one house rule by taking Red into his bedroom, so he figured he had nothing to lose by breaking another. He wanted his dog on the bed where he could lie down next to him and pet him and talk to him and make him feel safe.

Actually, Bruce needed that comfort as much as Red did. He had just been through the most frightening experience of his life, and he knew this was just the beginning. When his father got home from work, life would not be pleasant.

Unable to believe his good fortune, Red heaved himself up onto the mattress. Bruce collapsed against the pillows, stroking the dog's silky head and watching the shadow of the elm tree outside the bedroom window extend itself slowly across the opposite wall as the sun sank lower in the west. At one point, he heard his father's car pull into the driveway. Soon after that, he heard the phone ring. He was bracing himself to be summoned when the phone rang a second time.

"Here it comes," Bruce said softly to Red. He gave the dog one final pat and motioned him to the floor. He got off the bed himself and opened the door, and the two of them went quietly out into the hall.

Andi was poised at the top of the stairwell, eavesdropping.

"I wonder what Dad's so mad about," she whispered. She glanced at Bruce and Red and did a double take. "Did you have Red in your room? Mom will have a fit if she finds out."

"There's only one person who can tell her," Bruce said shortly. "Besides, she'll have a fit in a few seconds anyway. Wait till Dad's off the phone."

"I'm not going to tell," Andi assured him. "That's a stupid rule anyway. I sneak Bebe and Friday into my room all the time. I keep them shut in the closet until Mom's done kissing me good night, and then I let them out to sleep with me. Mom thinks they spend the night in the laundry room."

"You're lucky she doesn't do laundry in the evening," Bruce said. "What was Dad saying on the phone just now?"

But that question turned out to be unnecessary, as his father was suddenly shouting, "Bruce, come down here!"

"Take Red down the stairs to the kitchen and put him out in the yard," Bruce whispered urgently to Andi.

"What's going on?" Andi asked him.

"You'll find out soon enough," Bruce told her. "And you don't need to worry about running into Mom in the kitchen. There's no way she's still in there cooking; she's in the living room with Dad."

"Bruce!" Mr. Walker shouted impatiently.

"I'm coming," Bruce called back, but he paused long enough to make certain that Andi had a solid grip on Red's collar and was leading him down the hall to the stairs to the kitchen.

He knew that he was in for it the moment he entered the living room. His father looked both furious and worried, and his mother was seated on the sofa, obviously very upset.

"Is it true that you let Red Rover run out into traffic?" Mr. Walker demanded.

"It's not like I *let* him," Bruce said. "He got scared and bolted."

"And apparently caused a two-car accident. I've had calls from both drivers within the past five minutes. They claim there was damage to their vehicles and it was caused by Red Rover."

"I guess that's right," Bruce admitted. "They had to stop fast. But the reason Red ran out there —"

"You don't need to explain," Mr. Walker said. "I understand totally. Irish setters are excitable and can easily pull free of their handlers. That's one of the reasons we were hesitant about letting you have a large dog. We were afraid that you couldn't control him, and apparently you can't."

"Bruce, honey, it's *you* that we're worried about," said Mrs. Walker. Her face was pale and there was a tremor in her voice. "From what those drivers said, you could have been killed!"

"I'm fine, Mom," Bruce assured her. "And Red is, too. If it weren't for Jerry —"

"This has nothing to do with Jerry Gordon," his father said. "It has to do with a dog who has become unruly."

Mrs. Walker nodded in agreement. "Red has a sweet nature, but a dog that size doesn't fit with our lifestyle. Every boy who wants a dog should have one. But is there any reason that the dog can't be a small one? Perhaps Andi would let you have Friday."

"I don't want Friday!" Bruce exclaimed in horror.

"A dog is a dog," his mother said reasonably. "Friday's a dear little creature. You hardly even know she's around."

"I don't want Friday!" Bruce repeated. "I want Red Rover!"

"I wouldn't let Bruce have Friday if he wanted her!" Andi cried, bursting in through the doorway to the kitchen. To Bruce's relief, she had apparently accomplished her mission and put Red Rover in the yard. "You promised that Friday and Bebe could both be *my* dogs!"

"Children, stop this right now!" Mr. Walker commanded. "Can't you see you're upsetting your mother? Andi, there's no reason to get hysterical. Your mother just made a suggestion, and I personally think —"

The phone rang again, and he quickly snatched up the receiver. This time Bruce could hear every word of his father's side of the conversation, and it was all too clear what was being said on the other end of the line.

"That was Gerald Gordon," Mr. Walker said unnecessarily as he replaced the receiver on the hook. "Apparently his son was at the scene and saw what happened."

"I told you he was there," Bruce said. "He's the reason Red ran."

"Don't interrupt," his father said. "Mr. Gordon is concerned about the legal aspects of this situation. You haven't paid for Red Rover, so legally he is still the property of the Gordons. Apparently this time the drivers aren't going to press charges, but Mr. Gordon is worried, and with good reason, that he'll be held responsible if that dog gets away again and causes further problems."

"Did Mr. Gordon say he wants Red back?" Bruce asked fearfully.

"He didn't exactly demand it, but he did suggest it," his father told him. "He mentioned that Jerry is taller and stronger than you are and more physically capable of controlling a dog this size. But he's mostly concerned about his own liability. He wants you to either purchase Red Rover or return him. He says that Jerry has matured a lot in recent months. He's much more responsible than he used to be and is begging for a chance to prove himself."

"It's hard to earn money when you're only thirteen," Bruce said. "In another month I'll be able to get yard work, but now it's all I can do to keep Red in dog food."

"Dad, why don't you loan Bruce the money?" Andi suggested.

"That wasn't our agreement," Mr. Walker said firmly. "I allowed Bruce to keep Red Rover against my better judgment with the understanding that he would earn the money to purchase him. I envisioned this as a valuable learning experience. My handing him the money would defeat that purpose."

"I *will* earn the money!" Bruce said. "I give you my word, Dad. And I promise Red will never run off like that again."

"You're right about that," said Mr. Walker. "We have a fenced-in yard, and he can stay in it, just like your sister's dogs."

"You mean, I can't take him out for a run?" Bruce exclaimed.

"Not as long as he legally belongs to Mr. Gordon."

"But Red will go crazy cooped up all day!" Bruce protested.

"Don't push your luck," his father told him. "If I weren't so softhearted, I'd insist that you take that dog back to the Gordons right now, but I'm going to allow him to stay if he's confined to the yard. And as soon as school's out for the summer, which I believe is quite soon now, I expect you to find a way to pay off your debt. Now, both you kids, wash your hands and help your mother get dinner on. From the wonderful smell in this house, I believe we're having pot roast."

Bruce pulled Andi aside as she was headed for the bathroom.

"Okay, I'm in," he told her. "Let's publish a newspaper."

CHAPTER THREE

There were two unpleasant surprises waiting for Bruce when he attended the first editorial meeting on Saturday morning. One was that Andi was calling the paper *The Bow-Wow News.* The other was that, without bothering to consult him, she had asked her best friend, Debbie, to work as a reporter.

"That's a ridiculous name for a newspaper," Bruce objected. He couldn't very well complain about Debbie, since she was there at the meeting, taking notes on a pad of yellow paper. He had nothing against Debbie personally, but he knew how girls were; if the group had disagreements, Debbie would always side with Andi.

She immediately proved that by stating, "I think *The Bow-Wow News* is a marvelous name."

"And Debbie's already at work on the gossip column," Andi said. "She's written a piece about

Tiffany Tinkle's dog, Ginger. Remember, the one who had all those Bulldale puppies?"

"I remember, all right," Bruce said. "They were so funny looking that it took us weeks to find homes for them. Okay, Debbie, let's hear it. What's Ginger up to?"

Debbie cleared her throat and began to read from her notepad.

"Ginger Tinkle has again found romance after her breakup with Bully Bernstein, her childhood sweetheart. She's engaged to marry an Airedale named Prince Charming. Ginger's mistress, Tiffany, says Prince Charming has a pedigree and their children are going to be beautiful. Tiffany says Bully Bernstein was too immature for Ginger."

"Why does she think Bully's immature?" Andi asked her.

"It's the way he's been raised," said Debbie. "Tiffany says the Bernsteins spoil him. They treat him like a child, even now that he's a father."

"You mean they talk baby talk to him?" Andi asked uncomfortably. "There's nothing wrong with that. I sometimes call Bebe and Friday my 'itsy-bitsy doggies.' That has nothing to do with their maturity, it just makes them feel loved."

"That's not what I mean," Debbie said. "Bully sits in a high chair."

"He does *what*?" Bruce exclaimed, startled out of his boredom. "Why would anybody put a dog in a high chair?"

"To get him up to the table level," Debbie explained. "He eats at the table with the Bernsteins."

"I think we've got our first feature story!" Andi cried excitedly.

When they phoned the Bernsteins to set up an interview, the elderly couple was delighted. They were doubly thrilled when they learned that Bruce was going to take Bully's picture.

"What did you say your paper was called?" Mrs. Bernstein asked.

"*The Canine Gazette*," Bruce told her.

"It is *not*!" shrieked Andi, who was standing at his elbow. "It's *The Bow-Wow News*!" She snatched the receiver from his hand. "Did you hear that, Mrs. Bernstein? It's *The Bow-Wow News*! We took a vote, and Bruce lost."

"They're both nice names," Mrs. Bernstein said. "I just need to know what to tell people. I'm sure all our friends will want copies. Why don't you and your photographer come over about five this evening? That way you can photograph Bully having dinner."

The Bernsteins' home was a pretty, white-shingled house with neatly painted blue trim. The only thing odd about it was the wooden fence that stood between it and the Tinkles' house next door. It was the highest fence that Bruce and Andi had ever seen.

"Maybe the families don't like each other," Bruce commented.

"Or it might have to do with Ginger's breakup with Bully," Andi speculated. "If Ginger has another boyfriend, it may make Bully sad if he sees them together."

The knocker on the Bernsteins' front door was shaped like a bulldog, and the doorbell was set in a picture of a bulldog's face. To ring the bell, you had to push the dog's pink nose. Bruce pressed the nose and half expected to hear it bark. However, to his disappointment, it chimed like any other doorbell.

Mr. Bernstein answered the door. He was a small, stout man with a square-jawed face and a double chin and looked quite a bit like the door knocker.

Beyond him, on the sofa, a large brown bulldog was sprawled on his side in front of a wide-screen TV, watching *Lady and the Tramp*.

"This is Bully," Mr. Bernstein said, making introductions. "Bully, these are reporters from a local newspaper. They want to write an article and take your picture."

Bully didn't even roll his eyes in their direction.

"He's caught up in the story," Mr. Bernstein explained. "This is his favorite DVD. We always let him watch it while he's waiting for dinner. We don't approve of his watching TV in the evening. It's too stimulating right before bedtime, so we much prefer to read to him."

"That's so wise of you!" Andi said. "Bully will love our newspaper. All of the stories are for dogs."

Mrs. Bernstein had heard their voices and came bustling in from the kitchen, wiping her hands on her apron. She was short and round and smiley, exactly like her husband. The two of them and Bully made a perfect little family.

"What made you choose Bully for your very first issue?" Mrs. Bernstein asked them.

"Our reporter heard about him from your next-door neighbor," Andi said and immediately regretted the statement as she watched the woman's smile fade.

"That Ginger Tinkle, next door, is a floozy," Mrs. Bernstein said. "She developed a crush on Bully the first time she saw him. We used to have a wire fence between our houses, and she'd sit and flirt with Bully and make little whining sounds. Of course, Bully was intrigued, as any dog would be, so he made little whining sounds back at her just to be friendly. Then, one dreadful day, when Bully was out in the yard, not even making whining sounds, Ginger came over the fence. She just jumped right over it!"

"But the fence is so high!" Andi exclaimed.

"It wasn't back then. It was high enough to keep Bully from wandering, but Ginger's an Airedale. Have you ever seen Airedales jump? It's like they have springs in their feet. Ginger sailed over that fence as if it weren't there!"

"So you tore the fence down and rebuilt it?" Bruce asked with interest.

"It's the Tinkles who built that monstrosity," Mr. Bernstein told him. "A giraffe couldn't see over that fence if it was standing on its toes. There's no way of knowing what goes on in their backyard now."

"So Bully never even got to see his children," Mrs. Bernstein continued, picking up the story where she had left off. "The whole situation was terribly upsetting for him. Can you imagine the shock of having that great big creature suddenly land right next to him like a meteor falling out of the sky!"

"That must have been scary," Andi agreed. "And it's sad about the puppies. Bruce took some cute pictures if Bully wants to see them."

"You have pictures of Bully's children!" Mr. Bernstein exclaimed eagerly. "How did you come to take those?"

"We were helping Tiffany find homes for them," Andi told him. "Mr. Tinkle had threatened to drown them because they weren't purebreds."

"Oh, please, let's talk about pleasanter subjects," said Mrs. Bernstein. "The meat loaf should be done by now, and Bully's movie is almost over. He can watch the rest after dinner. Bruce, what a cute little camera! Does it take good pictures?"

"It takes digital pictures," Bruce said. "They're excellent quality. You can make them into prints or look at them on the computer."

"Bruce is a great photographer," Andi assured

them. "I know you'll be pleased with Bully's portrait."

"I hate to disturb you, Bully, but it's time to get washed up for dinner," Mrs. Bernstein said gently, giving the dog an affectionate pat on his haunches.

She switched off the DVD, and Bully sighed and rolled off the sofa.

"Meat loaf!" Mrs. Bernstein told him, and he seemed to brighten up a bit.

Mrs. Bernstein led the way into the dining room. The table was laid with three place settings. Bruce and Andi watched in fascination as Mrs. Bernstein got a washcloth and soap and carefully washed both of Bully's front paws. Then Mr. Bernstein lifted him into his high chair. The tray of the chair had been removed so it could be pushed up even with the table.

"Does he really use silverware?" Andi asked, eyeing the knife, fork, and spoon that were neatly arranged on Bully's place mat.

"Of course not," Mr. Bernstein said good-naturedly. "There's no way a dog could use silverware. He'd have to hold it in his teeth, and then how could he chew? It's just that the place mat would look rather odd with no silverware, and my wife likes to set a pretty table."

It *was* a pretty table, with silver candleholders and a centerpiece of purple pansies and long-stemmed goblets for ice water. Bruce was relieved to see that Bully didn't have a goblet. His water was served in a soup bowl.

Mr. Bernstein took his seat at the head of the table, and Mrs. Bernstein brought in the plates that she'd prepared in the kitchen. The meat loaf looked and smelled delicious.

"This will just take a minute," Bruce promised as he started snapping pictures. It was dark enough in the room so he had to use a flash, but Bully didn't seem to mind. His attention was focused entirely on his plate of meat loaf and mashed potatoes.

He licked his lips and leaned forward to rest his chins on the table. He had more of those than Mr. Bernstein, and when he squashed them down on the place mat they resembled a stack of pancakes.

"Mind your manners, dear," Mrs. Bernstein told him. "You know we don't start eating until we've said the blessing."

Everyone bowed their heads while Mr. Bernstein said grace.

As soon as he heard "Amen," Bully buried his face in his plate and started slurping.

Bruce was beginning to feel queasy.

"I've gotten my pictures," he said. "So I guess we'll be leaving."

"Are you sure you don't want to wait for dessert?" Mr. Bernstein asked him. "My wife's made a lemon meringue pie. That's Bully's favorite."

"Please, stay and enjoy it with us," said Mrs. Bernstein.

"Well," Andi began, "if you're sure —"

Bruce realized with horror that she was planning to say yes. Andi had never met any kind of pie she didn't like.

"We've got to get home," he said quickly. "Our parents will be wondering where we are. Thanks so much for letting us intrude on your mealtime. I'll try to find the snapshots I took of those puppies. Maybe Andi can arrange for Bully to visit them. She found most of the homes for them, so she knows where they live."

As soon as they were back on the sidewalk, he turned to Andi accusingly. "You were really planning to stay and eat at that table?"

"The table was lovely," Andi said. "And so are the Bernsteins. And, Bruce — it was *lemon meringue pie*!"

"That's just the point!" Bruce said. "Can you imagine what it would be like to sit across from Bully and watch him eat *that*? Mashed potatoes were bad enough. He even had them in his ears. But lemon meringue? Give me a break!"

"Mrs. Bernstein seems like a wonderful cook," Andi said. "I'm going to have Debbie ask her for the meat loaf recipe. A recipe column for dogs would be a great addition to the paper."

"A recipe column!" Bruce groaned. "Andi, I can't take this! You girls are running the show, and I feel like an outsider. Since you've brought Debbie on board as a reporter, I want my friend Tim to be the publisher. Tim knows all about computers. He can download a program that has columns and head-lines and sidebars so this won't look like a grade-school newspaper."

Andi was silent a moment, but he knew that he'd hooked her when she asked, "What's a sidebar?"

"You can leave that to Tim," Bruce said. "He'll make us look professional. If you want me to be your photographer, Tim's part of the package."

CHAPTER FOUR

The first one hundred copies of *The Bow-Wow News* rolled off of Tim's printer looking so professional that the four of them could hardly believe they had created it. The headline, "Bully Bernstein Loves Meat Loaf," ran across the top of the front page above Bruce's picture of Bully in his high chair. The flash from the camera had illuminated the dog's bulging eyes so they glistened like diamonds, and the stream of saliva at the corner of his mouth reflected the light from the candles on the beautifully set table.

Andi's article was centered beneath the photograph, and next to that, in a separate column, was Mrs. Bernstein's meat loaf recipe.

"That's a sidebar," Tim explained to Andi. "It's a box for extra information that goes with an article but isn't exactly part of it."

"It looks wonderful!" Andi exclaimed enthusiastically. "This is just like a paper you'd buy at a newsstand!"

Her resentment at having been blackmailed into having Tim as their publisher had been quickly erased when he had agreed with the girls on the name of the paper.

"I expected you to be on my side," Bruce had grumbled. "How can you agree to a name like that?"

"We want to sell papers," Tim said. "*The Canine Gazette* sounds so intellectual that people might worry that their dogs aren't smart enough to enjoy it."

"How much should we charge?" Andi asked him.

"Fifty cents is standard for newspapers," Tim said. Then, just as Bruce was getting irritated at the way his friend had walked right in and taken over, Tim went on to say, "I think we should agree right off the bat that all the money we make will go to Bruce until Red Rover is paid for. After that we can start dividing it up."

Neither of the girls objected to that suggestion, so Bruce made no more complaints about the name of the paper.

It had taken Tim several days to master the newspaper format, but now, at last, the first issue of *The Bow-Wow News* was right there in front of them. Its pages lay in neat stacks on Tim's computer desk, crisp and glossy and still slightly warm from the printer. Andi stroked the photo of Bully's face with her fingertips as lovingly as if she were stroking the heads of Bebe and Friday. Then she turned the sheet over to look at the second page, which contained a poem she had written called "Ginger's Heartbreak." The poem was about an Airedale whose master wanted to drown her puppies because they weren't purebreds. It started with the lines:

T'were just five little balls of fur,
But, oh, they meant so much to her!

Then, as an afterthought, Andi had added an additional verse about the puppies' father, who was denied visitation rights:

The fence between was high and mean
And not a puppy could be seen.

Every time she read those lines she felt a terrible sadness. Even though the Bulldale puppies had ended up in good homes, Ginger had found a new love, and Bully would soon see pictures of the puppies he had fathered, she still found the situation heart-wrenching. Because, what if there *hadn't* been a happy ending? What if Mr. Tinkle had followed through on his threat to drown those puppies, and Ginger had died of a broken heart, and Bully had lived a whole lifetime without ever learning what happened to the family he never had a chance to know? The mere thought of so much misery made her want to rush straight to her room and write another poem. But that would have to wait until the second issue. First they had to sell this first one.

They decided to conduct their sales in an organized manner by making a list of people they knew who owned dogs and working in pairs to visit all of them.

Tim suggested that each of the boys be partnered with a girl.

"People are more inclined to buy things from girls," he said. "My sisters sell tons of Girl Scout cookies, because they're little and cute and people can't say no to them. If Debbie and Andi could be cute, we'd make a lot of sales." He studied the girls for a moment and then said, "I'll go with Debbie."

"Thanks a bunch!" Bruce responded sarcastically, but he was actually relieved. At least with Andi, he knew what he was dealing with. He had no idea what he could expect from Debbie and what she might do to be cute. Anybody who volunteered to write a gossip column was the sort of person who made him nervous.

So he and Andi set off with fifty copies of the paper and, after a stop at home to sell a copy to their mother, continued on down to Aunt Alice's house at the end of the block. In recent months, every time Bruce had seen their great-aunt, he had found himself doing a double take. On the surface, she seemed no different from what she had always been — a sweet, fussy, white-haired lady who gardened and played bingo. It was only the past November that he and Andi had learned that, back in her younger days, Aunt Alice and her husband had run a detective agency. It was next to impossible for Bruce to incorporate those two images.

"A newspaper subscription!" Aunt Alice exclaimed when they explained the reason for their visit. "What an interesting coincidence! It's been months since anybody wanted to sell me a subscription, and now it's happened twice in one day!"

"Somebody else is selling a newspaper for dogs?" Andi asked in horror. "I thought we were the only ones!"

"I'm certain you are, dear," Aunt Alice said reassuringly. "Yours is the only dog newspaper I've ever heard of. Jerry Gordon and his cousin came by this morning selling subscriptions, but those were for magazines, not newspapers, and nothing on their list was about dogs. Has either of you met Connor?"

"No," Bruce said, "but I've heard about him."

"A delightful young man," Aunt Alice told them. "He looks a lot like Jerry. He's here in Elmwood for the summer, visiting the Gordons, and he and Jerry are raising money for charity by selling magazine subscriptions. I wasn't familiar with the titles, but they all sounded interesting."

"Did you subscribe to one?" Andi asked her.

"Yes, a magazine called *Happy Housekeeping*," Aunt Alice said. "And I definitely want to subscribe to *The Bow-Wow News*. How much is it?"

"Fifty cents for one issue or three dollars for the summer," Andi said, feeling a bit guilty, since she knew her aunt didn't own a dog. "You don't have to do this, Aunt Alice. We know you don't like dogs much."

"But I *do* like my great-niece and great-nephew," Aunt Alice said, beaming at them. "And it's not that I *dislike* dogs, it's just that I'm allergic to dog hair. I'll take a subscription for the summer. Just wait a teensy minute while I run and get my purse."

She disappeared into the house, and Andi whispered to Bruce, "Do you think she's packing a gun underneath that housecoat?"

"Of course not," Bruce whispered back. "That detective stuff was years ago, back when Uncle Peter was alive. That is, if it ever happened. Dad and Mom may have been kidding us."

Aunt Alice came bustling back with three one-dollar bills. She handed Andi the money and reached for a newspaper.

"Oh, my!" she gasped, catching sight of the front-page photo. "I know Mrs. Bernstein from Garden Club! What in the world is she doing?"

"Serving dinner," Andi told her, although she thought that was obvious. Mrs. Bernstein was holding a plate piled with meat loaf.

"Who's that in the high chair?" Aunt Alice asked. "Is that their grandchild?"

"That's Bully, their bulldog," Bruce told her. "Like it says in the headline, Bully loves meat loaf."

"I can't wait to read the story," Aunt Alice said, staring at the photo with fascination. She hurriedly kissed them both good-bye and rushed into the house.

"That went rather well," Andi remarked, fingering the crisp new bills.

However, the rest of their sales efforts weren't so productive. They sold a copy of the paper to Andi's fifth-grade teacher, who considered reading very important, and a copy to one of the families who had adopted a Bulldale. Beyond that, they weren't very successful. Almost everywhere they went they were told that Jerry Gordon and his cousin, Connor, had been there just ahead of them selling magazine subscriptions.

"I don't normally read many magazines, but when Connor described the ones on this particular list they sounded irresistible," one woman told them. "And half of all the money they make goes to charity."

It was late afternoon when they ended their route at the Bernsteins', where the huge wooden fence threw a shadow over half the front yard. The couple purchased ten copies to send to relatives. Their faces grew tender when Bruce gave them his snapshots of the Bulldales.

"That littlest one has Bully's eyes," Mrs. Bernstein said softly.

When she read "Ginger's Heartbreak" and came to the verse about Bully, her own eyes filled with tears.

"That poem is extraordinary," she told Andi. "I can't believe a mere child could describe Bully's feelings so perfectly. You've known him for such a short time, yet you captured his soul! And I never realized the depth of poor Ginger's feelings. I misjudged that sweet dog so badly. *'T'were just five little balls of fur'* — oh, poor Ginger!"

"We've got to go," Andi said, starting to tear up herself at the beauty of her poem.

"Not yet!" Mrs. Bernstein cried. "Bully would never forgive me if I didn't give you a little thank-you present."

She disappeared into the kitchen and came hurrying back with two slices of lemon meringue pie.

When they got back to Tim's house, he and Debbie were there waiting. They looked very pleased with themselves.

"So, how many copies did you sell?" Bruce asked them.

"All of them," Tim said with a grin.

"All *fifty*?" Bruce couldn't believe what he was hearing. "You mean, you got twenty-five dollars?"

"Would you believe twice that?" Tim said. He reached into his pocket and pulled out a check. "I asked my dad if we needed to set up a special bank account, but he said he doesn't think that's necessary. Andi can endorse the check over to you, and you can deposit it in your savings account. That can be our Red Rover Fund."

"But *fifty dollars*, all from one person?" Bruce exclaimed. He looked at the signature. "Margaret Tinkle. Isn't that Tiffany's mother? Don't tell me the Tinkles bought fifty copies of our paper and paid *a dollar apiece* for them?"

"It was Andi's poem," Debbie said. "They reacted to that strongly."

"Really?" Andi asked in amazement. She had seen how deeply her poem had affected the Bernsteins but had never imagined that it would have that effect on the Tinkles. Maybe her poem had softened their evil hearts. It was said that great writers had the power to influence their readers. If, at eleven years old, she could already do that, what incredible things might she accomplish when she was older? Her mind went sweeping across the years that lay ahead of her, and she saw herself quite clearly as an old, old woman of forty or so, getting out of bed in the morning and tottering straight to her computer to get to work changing people's lives for the better.

"Andi and I only sold fifteen copies," Bruce said. "That means we've got thirty-five left. Let's try to sell them out in front of the pet store."

"That wouldn't be legal," Debbie said.

"That was part of the deal we made with the Tinkles," Tim explained. "We can't sell any more copies of this first issue."

"What do you mean, we can't sell more copies?" Andi demanded. "We own *The Bow-Wow News*. We can sell as many copies as we want."

"No, we can't," Bruce told her, staring at the memo line on the check, on which Mrs. Tinkle had printed, *Payment in full for all rights to Andrea Walker's poem "Ginger's Heartbreak."* "When we deposit this check, your poem will belong to Mrs. Tinkle. We won't have the right to use it."

"They don't want people to read that poem," Debbie said. "It makes them sound like awful people, which, of course, they are. The extra twenty-five dollars was to stop us from selling more copies so their friends and neighbors won't see it."

"You shouldn't have agreed to that, Tim," Bruce said. "Not without asking Andi."

But to his surprise, Andi did not seem to be upset.

"Fifty dollars is a lot of money," she said. "I bet a lot of grown-up poets don't get that much. And I can always write other poems. I've got a pile of them stacked up inside me. All I have to do is pick up a pencil."

Her mind leapt ahead to their second issue:

Just five sweet, cuddly balls of fuzz,
But, oh, how hard the parting was!

Maybe the Tinkles would buy fifty copies of that one, too.

CHAPTER FIVE

Bruce first encountered Connor when he was on his way to Aunt Alice's house to deliver the second issue of the paper. Connor had just pulled into the driveway of the Gordons' house next door and was climbing out of a silver Miata, exactly the car Bruce dreamed of owning one day. It looked out of place next to Jerry's scuffed-up skateboard, which was positioned against the garage door in its usual attack mode.

Bruce's first reaction was a startled impression that he was looking at Jerry Gordon, four inches taller and twenty pounds heavier, and that Jerry had somehow managed to charm the people at the Department of Motor Vehicles into giving him a driver's license two years before he was eligible.

Then he immediately realized that this thought was ridiculous and the young man was Jerry's visiting cousin.

"Nice wheels!" Bruce said, for he felt he had to say something. The two of them were standing directly across from each other with just a small strip of lawn between them. "I'm Bruce Walker. I live a few houses down from here."

He braced himself for Connor's response, recalling with a shudder how unpleasant his first meeting with Jerry had been. The resemblance between the cousins was so remarkable that he felt as if he were meeting Jerry all over again.

But Connor gave him a friendly smile and came over with his hand extended.

"Thanks! I'm Connor Gordon," he said. "Aren't you and your sister the kids who are publishing a newspaper?"

"That's us," Bruce said, taking his hand and shaking it. Connor's grip was firm and self-confident and his smile seemed genuine. "How did you know about the paper?"

"Word gets around," Connor said. "I'd like to subscribe. How much is it?"

"Three dollars for the summer," Bruce told him. "Do you own a dog?"

"No, but I wish I did," Connor said, pulling out his wallet and counting the money. "Jerry tells me he used to have a setter, but it ended up with you. I'm sure there's a story behind that."

"There is," Bruce said, but he didn't offer to elaborate. "I guess you're aware that I'm not exactly Jerry's favorite person."

"That's what I gathered," Connor said with a sympathetic chuckle. "My cousin's basically a good kid, but he can sometimes be a pill. That's the reason Uncle Gerald invited me to visit. He thought I'd be a good influence."

"Lots of luck!" Bruce said. "Here, take a copy of this current issue. The paper's a weekly, so I'll deliver the next one next Wednesday."

"Sounds good," Connor said. "I'm looking forward to reading them. You and your sister must have good heads for business; you've zeroed in on a hot market." He gave Bruce a friendly clap on the shoulder. "Good to meet you, bud. I'll see you around."

"So long," Bruce said. "And thanks for subscribing to the paper."

Connor loped back across the driveway and disappeared into the Gordons' house, and Bruce continued on to Aunt Alice's, disconcerted by the friendly exchange. Connor could have been Jerry's clone as far as looks went, but his personality was so different that it had been like talking to Jerry, yet *not* talking to Jerry, or like talking to Jerry when he was pretending to be somebody else.

"I just met Connor Gordon," Bruce told Aunt Alice when she opened the door to him. "I didn't realize Jerry's cousin was old enough to drive."

"Apparently so," Aunt Alice said. "He's very mature, and he doesn't let any grass grow under his feet. He's been here only a week, and it's amazing the way he's made himself a part of the community. Every morning and evening he's off doing volunteer work, and when he's not working, he and Jerry go door-to-door selling their magazine subscriptions. Busy, busy, busy!"

She eagerly reached for the paper, but her face drooped in disappointment when she saw the front-page photo.

"That's definitely not Bully Bernstein."

"No," Bruce said. "That's Snowflake Swanson. She's a very important dog. She's been winning beauty contests for over eight years. The Swansons have her insured for fifty thousand dollars."

"That must be why she's wearing a crown," Aunt Alice commented. "Does she always stick her nose in the air like that?"

"She's vain about her looks," Bruce acknowledged. "She goes to the beauty parlor every week to get her nails done. But there's a lot of other stuff in this issue if Snowflake doesn't interest you. There's an article about how to pull ticks off dogs without popping them. That can be very tricky. And there's a new poem by Andi called 'Virginia's Tragedy.'"

"Well, that should keep me occupied," Aunt Alice said. "But I'd love to read more about Bully."

The second fifty-dollar sale to the Tinkles that Andi had anticipated did not materialize. Mrs. Tinkle seemed irritated by the suggestion. "I'm not concerned about 'Virginia's Tragedy,'" she told Andi. "None of our friends will recognize Ginger by that name."

However, Snowflake Swanson's owners bought six copies because they loved Snowflake's picture, and Dr. Bryant, the veterinarian who owned the Bryant Pet Clinic, was so impressed by the article about tick removal that he bought fifty copies to use as handouts for his patients.

"Summer is tick season," he told Bruce. "Every pet owner should have this important information."

But the newspaper's strongest selling point was turning out to be the gossip column. Every pet owner whose dog was mentioned in that column bought multiple copies, and several took out subscriptions.

"I've got to find a way to get more gossip," Debbie said at their weekly editorial meeting. "I've used up all of my sources. Tiffany Tinkle won't talk to me since we printed that poem about Ginger, and my other friends won't tell me anything about their dogs except how sweet they are. A gossip columnist's life is not as easy as you'd think."

"You need a new territory," Tim told her. "What about the Doggie Park?"

Debbie regarded him blankly.

"It's over on Oak Street," Tim said. "That big grassy area with the fence around it. It's a park where people can let their dogs off their leashes. I took my dog, MacTavish, there once, and the dogs were having a great time playing together. Mac would have loved to go back, but I couldn't stand it. It was filled with a bunch of overweight women sitting on benches and yammering to each other while their dogs got all the exercise."

"That sounds perfect!" Debbie exclaimed. "Would they let me in without a dog? I don't own one, because Mom is so devoted to her cat."

"You can borrow Bebe," Andi offered. "Friday's too shy to enjoy that, but Bebe's very sociable."

"No, take MacTavish!" Tim pleaded. "He's dying to go back."

"I'll take turns," Debbie said. "First Bebe, then MacTavish. I can wear disguises and, with two different dogs, nobody will suspect I'm the same person."

So, the following day, Debbie came by to pick up Bebe to go to the Doggie Park. It cost a dollar to get in — "There are always business expenses," Tim reminded them — but she returned with a notebook filled with such interesting information that it was more than worth the entrance fee. Andi's eyes widened as she read Debbie's notes:

Trixie Larkin's master brings Trixie to the Doggie Park on his motorcycle. Trixie is learning how to make turn signals with her paw.

Fifi Anderson's mistress has a crush on Dr. Bryant. Sometimes she takes Fifi to his clinic, pretending Fifi has a stomachache even though she really doesn't.

Foxy Roper tried to bite a turtle and broke two front teeth. He's had five hundred dollars' worth of dental work.

Curly Roskin's owner smokes cigarettes, and Curly reeks of secondhand smoke. Curly has emotional problems because other dogs don't want to be around him.

Frisky Mason's owner is thinking about getting a second dog. She's told her friends, but she hasn't told Frisky, because she thinks Frisky will be jealous. But this reporter spotted Frisky hiding under a bench, eavesdropping. Frisky's no dummy. FRISKY KNOWS!!!

The father of Bebe and Friday Walker's owner is taking his wife to Europe.

Andi was stunned by that final item.

"My parents aren't going to Europe!"

"Yes, they are," Debbie said. "Foxy's owner works for a travel agency. She was telling Fifi's owner about how your dad came in and booked reservations for a three-week tour. They're going to France and Italy and Switzerland and London."

"Just them — not Bruce and me?"

"Just the two of them, to celebrate their fifteenth anniversary. It's a surprise for your mom. Your dad said she's always dreamed of going to Europe. They wanted to do it on their honeymoon, but they couldn't afford it. Now they can."

"I think that's terrific!" Bruce said. "Mom deserves a treat. It wasn't easy for her to pull up roots and move when Dad got his job transfer. But she never complained about leaving her own job and all of her friends. She just smiled all the time like it was a great adventure."

"But what about us?" Andi cried. "We'll be stuck with Aunt Alice!"

"We can stand it for three weeks," Bruce said.

"But the dogs —"

"They'll be right down the street. We'll be over there all the time except when we're sleeping. We couldn't go off and leave our new business anyway." He regarded his sister apprehensively. "Don't you dare tell Mom or blab to Dad that we know. And, Debbie, you can't put that information in your gossip column. This is Dad's surprise for Mom, and he's got to be the one to break the news. We don't want to ruin it for him."

Andi nodded unhappily. "I won't say anything, but I don't want to stay with Aunt Alice. I want to sleep with my dogs, and I don't want to live next door to Jerry for three weeks. Every time we step out the door he'll run us over with his skateboard."

"I don't think we have anything to worry about," Bruce told her. "I mean, of course you can't sleep with Bebe and Friday, but we won't be attacked by Jerry. His cousin, Connor, isn't going to let that happen."

"Have you met Connor?" Tim asked him. "I haven't had a chance to yet, but I've seen him driving around in his silver bullet. That sure is a cool car!"

"Connor's cool, too," Bruce said. "He looks like Jerry, but he isn't nasty at all. In fact, the whole reason he's here is to straighten Jerry out."

Bruce was disappointed that the Miata was not in the driveway when he stopped by the following Wednesday to deliver Connor's paper. He'd been looking forward to having another chance to talk with him and possibly even to beg a ride in his car.

But apparently Connor and Jerry were off somewhere together, because it was Mr. Gordon who came to the door.

"Please give this to Connor," Bruce said, handing him the paper. "And this is for you, sir — an installment payment on Red Rover."

"Fifty dollars!" Mr. Gordon exclaimed. "That's a sizable amount, Bruce, especially in comparison to your usual five-dollar payments. Jerry told me he thought you might be planning to default and return Red Rover, but obviously he was wrong."

"He was," Bruce said. "I am definitely buying Red Rover."

"If you have any thoughts to the contrary, don't feel committed," Mr. Gordon told him. "At the time I agreed to sell you the dog, Jerry was not at his best. But that's how teenagers are, and I've now come to realize that he's basically a good kid who got off on the wrong track. I think he was probably running with the wrong companions. Bad influences are a danger to vulnerable young people, and sometimes it takes a family effort to get them back on track. Jerry will be busy doing things with his cousin this summer. You've obviously met my nephew?"

"Yes," Bruce said. "He seems like a very nice guy."

"He's a charmer," Mr. Gordon agreed. "Connor's home is in Chicago, but his parents wanted him to spend the summer here in Elmwood. They thought that a small-town atmosphere would be a nice change for him."

"I'm sure it will," Bruce said politely, both startled and impressed by how smoothly Mr. Gordon was concealing Connor's true reason for being there. "Aunt Alice says Connor's doing a lot of volunteer work as well as selling magazine subscriptions."

"I'm very much in favor of his volunteer work," said Mr. Gordon. "It's a marvelous thing for young people to give of themselves to the community. However, you're mistaken about the magazine subscriptions. Connor sold magazines in Chicago, but he doesn't do that now."

"He doesn't?" Bruce exclaimed in surprise. "But Aunt Alice told me — a lot of people told me —"

"They're mistaken," Mr. Gordon said firmly. "Connor is not selling magazine subscriptions here in Elmwood. So, what about you, Bruce? What's the source of this large payment? A summer job mowing lawns?"

"Better than that," Bruce told him. If Mr. Gordon could stretch the truth a bit, he could, too. "I'm working as a photographer for the hottest new publication in town."

CHAPTER SIX

HERO DOG SAVES FAMILY

Trixie Larkin is a hero. When she smelled something funny in the night, Trixie barked.

"She didn't have to do that," Mrs. Larkin said. "She could have run out her doggie door. But Trixie barked and woke us up, and we called the fire department."

The fire department came. The thing that smelled funny was in the garbage disposal. It was not a fire.

"But it could have been a fire," Mrs. Larkin said. "If it had been a fire, we would have burned up if Trixie hadn't barked. I will never again feel safe if Trixie isn't with us."

Newspaper sales took a downhill slide when the story about Trixie was the lead article. It seemed that people weren't interested in a smoke-detecting dog who didn't detect smoke.

"That's cheating," complained one dissatisfied customer, who had bought the issue because of the photograph of Trixie wearing a firefighter's hat with a medal that said "World's Best Dog." Bruce was proud of that picture. He had purchased the child-size fire helmet at a toy store and created the medal with aluminum foil and a felt marker. But he had to admit that, in a way, it *was* cheating, because the thing in the garbage disposal hadn't been worth barking about. It had been a piece of fish. He offered to give the customer her money back, but she decided to keep the issue because of Andi's article about how to make your own flea powder.

"We've got to find more interesting subjects," Tim said. "What we need is another Bully Bernstein."

"Bully Bernsteins don't grow on trees," Bruce retorted. "We're going to wait a long time before we find another Bully."

"How *did* you find him?" Tim asked.

"Debbie learned about him from Tiffany," Bruce said. "The Tinkles were mad at the Bernsteins, and Tiffany was ranting to Debbie about how immature Bully was and let it drop about the high chair. If it hadn't been for that, we wouldn't have known about him."

"We need to find more dog owners who are mad at other dog owners," Tim said. "There must be a lot of them out there. But how do we get them stirred up enough to squeal on each other?"

"We could run an ad," Debbie suggested. She was wearing one of her disguises, because as soon as the meeting was over she was headed for the Doggie Park. This particular disguise involved hair extensions that belonged to her mother and a pair of false eyelashes. Bruce thought she looked ridiculous.

"Maybe we could offer a free subscription for tips about interesting stories," she continued as she practiced fluttering the lashes.

It was not a bad idea, even coming from Debbie, and they were mulling it over when the phone rang. A moment later, Mrs. Walker appeared in the doorway.

"It's for you, Andi," she said. "I didn't recognize the voice. I assume it's one of your subscribers."

Mr. and Mrs. Walker both thought their paper was adorable, although they didn't take it seriously as a source of income.

Andi picked up the receiver.

"*The Bow-Wow News,*" she said in a businesslike voice. "This is the editor speaking." She sat for a moment in silence and then asked, "Is there a particular time of day when this happens?" Listening intently, she reached for her notebook and began taking notes. "We'll get right on this, and thank you so much for informing us."

When she hung up the phone, she was beaming.

"We've got a scoop! Bruce, this will be your first major photo assignment!"

"What do you mean, my first assignment?" Bruce demanded. "I photographed Bully, Ginger, Snowflake, and Trixie. Don't they count?"

"I said *major* assignment. An investigative news story! That tipster owns one of the Bulldales. She's informing on another dog owner. She said Mr. Murdock, who lives two houses down from her, has a fox terrier named Barkley. Three times a day the Murdocks walk Barkley around the neighborhood, and *Mr. Murdock doesn't carry a pooper-scooper*!"

"My dad knows Mr. Murdock from the Rotary Club," Tim said. "He's vice president of the bank. Nobody messes with Mr. Murdock. If we publish something like that, he'll sue us for libel."

"Libel means 'lies,'" Andi said. "It isn't libel if it's true. We'll have to furnish proof, but that won't be a problem. Not if Bruce gets a picture."

"A picture of a man walking a dog without a pooper-scooper?" Tim protested. "He'll slide out of that one easily. He'll say Barkley didn't need to go, and there was nothing to scoop."

"But a picture is worth a thousand words," Andi said. "If one of those words begins with p —"

"Okay, I get it," Bruce said. "When does he do this?"

"Mr. Murdock walks Barkley at eight in the morning," Andi said, referring to her notes. "Mrs. Murdock walks him in the afternoon, but she carries a scooper. Mr. Murdock walks him for a final time after dinner. When do you think would be the best time to get a picture?"

"Not after dinner," Bruce said. "The light won't be good. Not the afternoon walk, because Mrs. Murdock obeys the law. So it will have to be in the morning. That's the best time anyway. Barkley will have been inside all night."

"I'll write a draft of the story," Andi said. "When you get back with the picture, we'll fill in the details, like exactly where and when it happened."

Bruce had a hard time sleeping that night, and between spells of wakefulness he dreamed. Each time he dozed off, the same dream started over, like a defective DVD that wouldn't stay in place when you hit the PAUSE button.

He dreamed about taking Red for a predawn run. At the start, they ran in darkness, but soon that lessened, and trees and houses began to take shape around them. The sky in the east turned pink and then orange and then gold, and the sun came bursting over the edge of the horizon. Red Rover was a wild thing, first dashing ahead, then rushing back to Bruce, practically dancing with joy as he stretched out his long, lean muscles and raced like a flaming arrow straight into the path of the rising sun.

In the dream, as in real life, Bruce had a plastic bag in his pocket and carried a pooper-scooper.

The final time he awakened, the sky outside his window had grown light enough so he could make out the branches of the elm tree. He lay there, listening to the chirping of the birds and feeling an almost irresistible urge to take Red running and sneak him back in the yard before his parents woke up.

But he couldn't make himself do it. Bruce was an honorable boy, and when he made a promise he kept it.

This can't go on, he told himself. *I've got to finish paying for Red.*

He got up and dressed and, although it was too early, slung his camera strap around his neck and walked the three blocks to the street where the Murdocks lived. In the hush of early morning, the sky turned pink and orange and gold, and he had a mystical sense that he was still dreaming. Except in the dream, Red Rover had been there with him. It seemed strange to be out at this hour alone.

Of course, he didn't have to be alone. Tim had offered to go with him. In fact, they all had wanted to go. But Bruce had insisted that he had to do this by himself if he was going to get a picture. There weren't many people on the sidewalks at that time of morning, and the ones who were there stood out. One boy, half-hidden behind a clump of bushes, might get by unnoticed, but a group of four children, staring and giggling (he knew that the girls would giggle, even though they swore that they wouldn't), couldn't help but attract Mr. Murdock's attention. And it might be disconcerting to Barkley, who was used to having the sidewalk to himself at that hour.

It was a long wait, but 8 A.M. finally arrived. It arrived and passed without any indication of life from within the Murdock house. Nobody even bothered to come out and get the newspaper.

The minute hand of Bruce's watch crept to 8:05, then to 8:10, then to 8:15. By 8:22, he was ready to give up and go home, when the door to the Murdock house suddenly flew open and a man and a dog stood framed in the doorway. Mr. Murdock was wearing a business suit and carrying a briefcase. He plucked the paper from the lawn and tossed it, along with the briefcase, through the open window of the shiny black Lexus in the driveway. Barkley was small and white, with one brown ear and a stub of a tail that wasn't wagging. He didn't look like a dog who was out to have fun. He looked like a dog on a mission.

Bruce had positioned himself across the street from the house in the shadow of an oak tree. The tipster hadn't told Andi which direction Mr. Murdock would take, so Bruce held back and waited until he saw the man turn right. Then he turned in that direction also and kept pace with him as he strode along the sidewalk. Mr. Murdock had a stern face, bristly gray hair, and a gray mustache that was perched above a mouth that didn't look like it smiled much. He clearly was not enjoying this time with his dog. He wanted to get this over with so he could go to work and read his newspaper.

Bruce made a mental note of the fact that he was not carrying a pooper-scooper.

When Mr. Murdock reached the corner, he turned right again, so Bruce was forced to cross the street and fall into step behind him. They continued on to the next corner, where Mr. Murdock again turned right and Bruce did likewise. They were already halfway around the block and Barkley hadn't even lifted his leg. He just kept marching along like a little white robot. Bruce found himself wondering if this was, in fact, a real dog, or if it might be one of those realistic battery-operated dogs that people sold in shopping malls.

But no, Barkley had to be real. Mr. Murdock was not a playful enough man to take a toy dog for a walk. He kept glancing impatiently at his watch and mumbling things to Barkley that Bruce wasn't close enough to hear. In fact, Bruce was starting to worry that he wasn't close enough to get a picture if something newsworthy did occur.

He quickened his pace to close the distance between them just as Mr. Murdock took another right turn at the corner — and then *it happened*! Barkley went into squat position. The angle could not have been better. Bruce had not yet started to turn the corner himself, so he was not exactly behind Barkley, but kitty-cornered to him, and could aim his camera across a flower bed. He clicked the shutter over and over and then zoomed back to include Mr. Murdock in the picture as he urged the dog to hurry and then yanked the leash to jerk him away from the evidence.

Bruce continued clicking frame after frame, too exhilarated to think about stopping. All caution about his own safety had been thrown to the winds and he had no thought for anything except his assignment. *This must be what it is like,* he thought, *to be a war correspondent, standing on the edge of a battlefield, immune to the dangers all around you, intent only on getting your story.*

He took a step forward to frame a shot with a spray of hydrangea. The dainty blue blossoms made an interesting contrast to the brown-and-white dog and the gray-and-white man.

Mr. Murdock gave the dog's leash another hard yank, and then he raised his eyes and looked straight at Bruce. For a moment he stared at him blankly. Then his eyes began to bulge and his mouth flew open.

"What the devil do you think you're doing?" he bellowed.

Bruce started running. He wished Red Rover were with him, because Red would have loved this. He had never run so fast before in his life.

Later, at Tim's house, the four of them gathered around Tim's computer as Bruce displayed one image after another.

"You sure took a lot of pictures," Tim said. "I can't believe you hung around that long."

"Time stood still," Bruce told him. "I was so caught up in it — tracking my subjects, looking for just the right angle. I know now for sure what I'm going to do for a living. I'm going to be a photojournalist."

"The close-ups are great," Debbie said. "You zoomed right in."

"But just on the dog," Andi said. "They're all great pictures, but Mr. Murdock isn't in them."

Bruce continued to click through the pictures until they gasped in unison, "That's the one!"

It was the final picture he had taken, framed with lacy blue flowers. Barkley had finished his business, and Mr. Murdock was jerking him forward. Bruce had snapped it at the exact moment Mr. Murdock spotted him. The man's face was contorted with fury. His left hand held Barkley's leash, and his right hand was aimed at Bruce as if he held a pistol. Neither hand held a pooper-scooper.

"That one's perfect!" Andi said.

CHAPTER SEVEN

The fourth issue of *The Bow-Wow News* sold out so quickly that Tim had to run a second printing. Everybody in town was discussing the story about Barkley. Then, to Andi's astonishment, she began to be contacted by people wanting to buy advertising space. The first was the pet store, which wanted to advertise a line of pooper-scoopers that worked like battery-operated vacuum cleaners. Then an organization called Concerned Citizens for Clean Neighborhoods contacted her about placing a campaign ad for a member of their group who was running for the town council.

But the third call was far less pleasant. It was from Mr. Murdock, who was threatening a lawsuit for invasion of privacy. Andi, who was alone in the house at the time, picked up the receiver and then wished that she had checked caller ID.

"That was libel!" Mr. Murdock exploded. "That lump on the sidewalk was a stone!"

"Our photographer assured us he saw Barkley do it," Andi said defensively.

"Your photographer is a liar!" Mr. Murdock bellowed and let loose a stream of swear words that caused Andi to cringe. She had never heard anybody use such language before.

It took tremendous effort to keep her voice steady.

"We'll consult with our legal advisor and get back to you," she said.

Then she hung up the phone and burst into tears.

Andi was truly scared. What legal advisor could she consult? It certainly couldn't be her parents. If they thought their children were in trouble, they wouldn't leave the country, and now that Andi had adjusted to the idea, she wanted them to go. They were wonderful parents and deserved a special celebration. She didn't know of many families where the parents had been married for fifteen years to the same people they started out with.

She had even adjusted to the thought of three weeks with Aunt Alice — as long as she could make frequent visits to Bebe and Friday.

Now, as she thought of Aunt Alice, it suddenly occurred to her that she might be a possible resource. As a former private investigator, she must know about the law. Maybe she could serve as a legal advisor.

Andi wiped her eyes and dialed her great-aunt's phone number. As always, it took her some time to get to the phone.

"Hello," she said, puffing a little as if she had raced in from the yard. Andi could picture her plopping down in the chair next to the telephone table with her garden shears still clutched in one pudgy hand.

"It's Andi, Aunt Alice," Andi told her. "I've got a question for you. A professional question, just between the two of us. Would that be all right?"

"Of course, dear," Aunt Alice said readily. "Off the record it will be." And then she surprised Andi by saying the last thing she expected to hear. "I imagine Mr. Murdock is threatening to sue *The Bow-Wow News*. Am I correct?"

Andi gasped. "How did you know?"

"I was sure he would when I saw his expression in the picture," Aunt Alice said. "Also, I've met that man at various social functions, and he doesn't have an easygoing nature. So, your question is, does he have grounds for a lawsuit?"

"Yes," Andi said faintly.

"Not if the photo was taken on public property and won't be used for commercial purposes," Aunt Alice said. "In other words, you are free to print it in your paper, but you can't sell it to people to use in advertisements. Does that help?"

"It helps a lot," Andi said. "As a matter of fact, a pet store wants to advertise pooper-scoopers. Their ad is scheduled for our next issue. Should we tell them we can't print it?"

"You can print it," said Aunt Alice. "Advertisements are how publications make money. Just don't link the ad to the picture of Mr. Murdock. Especially if you start selling your paper off the Internet, which I imagine is what you'll do next."

"We hadn't thought about that," Andi said. "But thank you."

"Anytime, dear," Aunt Alice said placidly.

By the time Andi hung up the phone, she was feeling much better.

"I can't believe you actually called Aunt Alice!" Bruce exclaimed when Andi described what had happened. "Do you think she'll blab to Mom and Dad?"

"I'm certain she won't," Andi told him. "Our consultation was off the record. She was wonderful, Bruce! It was like she was a whole different person! This must have been what she was like when she was a detective and was working on kidnappings and murders."

"Have you called Mr. Murdock back yet?" Bruce asked her.

"No," Andi said. "I just can't. Will you please call him? If he yells more rude things at me, I'm afraid I'll cry, and that's so unprofessional."

"Okay, I'll do it," Bruce agreed reluctantly. He had no more desire to talk to Mr. Murdock than Andi did, but he was, after all, the person who had taken the picture.

He dialed the Murdocks' number and, to his relief, got the answering machine.

"Murdock residence!" Mr. Murdock's voice roared at him. In the background he could hear Barkley yapping nervously and a woman's voice calling, "Please, dear, try to sound a little more welcoming!"

"Leave your message at the sound of the beep,"

Mr. Murdock snarled, ignoring his dog and wife as if neither existed.

The beep was so long in coming that it was obvious that the Murdocks had a lot of messages on their machine. Bruce wondered if they had stopped answering the phone because of an overload of calls from members of Concerned Citizens for Clean Neighborhoods.

When the beep did finally come, he said, "I'm Bruce Walker, the photographer who took the picture of you and Barkley. If you ever call us again, please ask to speak to me, not to my little sister. We've discussed the situation with our legal advisor, and she says there's nothing you can sue us for." He paused, uncertain about how to end the one-sided conversation. He didn't like to be rude and just hang up, but he didn't want to make idle chitchat either. He compromised by saying, "Have a nice day."

Despite the barrage of sales for the issue about Barkley, sales for the following issue were disappointing. Even regular customers weren't eager to purchase the newspaper, because they had now subscribed to *Dogs' Home Journal*, a new publication on Connor and Jerry's subscription list.

"Half of their money goes to charity," people told the children, although when asked which charity it was, they didn't seem certain.

"What a horrid thing for those boys to do!" Andi cried angrily. "We were here first! Jerry and Connor are copycats!"

"That's how business works," Tim said. "They saw we were on to something good and jumped on the bandwagon. There's nothing illegal about that, though it is sort of crummy. And it sure is messing up our sales."

"I'm sure Jerry's the one behind it," Bruce said. "I bet Connor doesn't even know about it. He's probably gotten so busy with all his volunteer work that he's let Jerry take over the business. That must be what Mr. Gordon meant when he told me Connor's no longer selling magazines."

He phoned Aunt Alice to ask what she knew about *Dogs' Home Journal*.

"Nothing specific," she said. "Just that it sounded like a nice magazine when Jerry described it. He came by a few days ago with a new subscription list. I told him I have all the reading matter I can keep up with, or I *will* have as soon I start getting *Happy Housekeeping*. It's certainly taking a long time for that subscription to be activated."

Bruce typed the title *Dogs' Home Journal* into an Internet search engine and didn't come up with any matches. However, the word "dogs" took him to dozens of message boards for people who liked to chat about their pets. One of them wanted to know how to make her own flea powder. Bruce helpfully posted an excerpt from Andi's article and added the fact that it came from *The Bow-Wow News*. Somebody else then asked, "Is that newspaper online?" and Bruce responded, "Not yet." Then, before he hit the SEND button, he impulsively added, "Watch this board for further developments."

When he described the exchange to Tim, his friend's freckled face lit up like a Christmas tree.

"What a great idea!" he exclaimed. "We can build a Web site! My dad has one for his business, and I'm sure he'll let us use his domain name and Internet provider."

The girls were not so enthusiastic.

"Aunt Alice suggested we put our paper online," Andi said. "But I don't understand what good it will do us if everyone reads it for free."

"I don't either," said Debbie. Today she was dressed in her second disguise, the one she wore on the days she went out with MacTavish. This outfit consisted of black jeans and an oversize black T-shirt. With dark glasses, and her curls tucked up under a baseball cap, it was almost impossible to tell if she was a girl or a boy. "If the paper is on the Internet, why would people buy it?"

"We won't put the whole paper on the site," Bruce said. "We'll post the first half of the articles and tell people that if they want to read the rest they'll have to send us fifty cents."

"It would cost that much for the envelope and stamp," Andi objected.

"The people who contact us will have computers," Tim said. "We can send them the rest of the paper as e-mail attachments and it won't cost us anything."

It took Tim most of a week to construct the Web site, and his father had to help quite a lot.

"It was harder than I thought, but Dad was terrific," Tim said. "With so many kids in our family, he and I don't get to do much together, just the two of us, so this was great. Andi, Dad says to tell you that he loved your last poem — the one about the dog who went swimming and got hit by a torpedo."

"He did?" Andi exclaimed with delight. That poem was one of her favorites. "Is the Web site finished? When can we start posting articles?"

"It's ready to roll," Tim told them. "Let's start with our most popular story."

"That's Bully!" they all said together. "Either that or Barkley."

"Let's make it Bully," Tim said. "Mr. Murdock needs time to simmer down. Bruce, can you make the picture fill the whole screen?"

"Sure," Bruce said. "And I can do stuff with photo enhancement. For instance, I can make the meat loaf stand up higher on the plate so people can see it better. And I can make Bully's drool reflect the flowers on the table." His heart was beating fast with the thrill of this new challenge.

The first online edition of *The Bow-Wow News* received more attention than they could have imagined, especially after Bruce posted information about the Web site on all the dog-lover message boards.

The enhanced photo of Bully with his heaping plate of food and stream of rainbow saliva delighted the Bernsteins.

"But why did you leave out the recipe?" Mrs. Bernstein asked them. "Everybody I know wants my meat loaf recipe."

"They can get it," Andi assured her. "But they'll have to send us fifty cents. Mrs. Bernstein, this is a *business*!"

Her decision to chop off the story at exactly the point where Mrs. Bernstein was preparing to reveal her recipe turned out to be a stroke of genius. Over two hundred people, including a chef at a restaurant in Atlanta, sent e-mail requests for an address where they could send their money. After a bit of discussion, Debbie agreed to have the payments sent to her house. Since both her parents worked, she could intercept the mail before they got home. As proud as they were of their success, Bruce and Andi were concerned that a sudden flood of envelopes addressed to *The Bow-Wow News* might be disconcerting to their parents, who still hadn't broken the news about their upcoming trip.

"Don't you think it's odd that they haven't told us yet?" Andi asked Bruce. "How long do you think they're going to wait?"

"As long as they can," Bruce said. "They're probably afraid you'll throw a fit about having to stay with Aunt Alice, so they're putting off telling us for as long as possible."

"I'm not going to do that," Andi said. "I feel differently about Aunt Alice now that she's our legal advisor."

Actually, her change in attitude went deeper than that, though she couldn't quite put her finger on what it was. Sometimes in the afternoons when she wasn't working on the paper she walked down the street to Aunt Alice's house to visit with her for twenty minutes or so. Twenty minutes was pretty much all she could handle, because Aunt Alice wasn't the same when she blathered away in her usual manner as when she spoke as "a professional." But now that Andi knew that another Aunt Alice was buried somewhere inside there, a fascinating core of — she wasn't sure what to call it, but something exciting and tough and strange, concealed underneath the wrinkles and soft sagging arms and dimpled cheeks — she wanted to be there when it reemerged. It was like having had a tiny glimpse of a magical image that dissolved into nothing, and sometimes you wondered if you'd ever really seen it.

But it *hadn't* dissolved. She was sure it was in there somewhere. And that certainty was what made her say to Bruce, "I'm actually looking forward to staying with Aunt Alice."

CHAPTER EIGHT

As they waited eagerly for the envelopes to start arriving, Tim's e-mail in-box was overflowing. One message was particularly interesting because it involved the recipe for Bully's favorite meat loaf.

A veterinarian in Ohio wrote, "If this meat loaf for dogs includes people-food, it might be dangerous for dogs who are allergic to such ingredients."

A man who owned a company that prided itself on manufacturing "the purest canned dog food in the world" suggested that they substitute his product for any un-doggly ingredients in Mrs. Bernstein's recipe.

"Concoctions that contain cereal products, onions, and tomato paste might upset a dog's digestive track," he wrote.

"I've been wondering about that," Bruce said to Andi when he read that e-mail. "Back when you were tossing bread crusts to Bebe and Friday, I told you I didn't think that was a good idea. I've read that dogs shouldn't be given people-food. We sure don't want to do anything to make dogs sick."

"That dog food guy offered to pay us to revise the recipe," Tim said. "Why don't we take out some of the people-food ingredients and replace them with his dog food?"

"That won't be a problem," Andi said. "I'll just make a few substitutions in the e-mail attachment. We won't have to change the Web site. We'll just send the recipe to people who ask for it, and we'll call it 'Bully's Extra-Healthy Meat Loaf with No Bad Things in It.'"

The first of the envelopes started arriving on Monday. Debbie waited for the letter carrier out by the mailbox with a coaster wagon so she could haul the envelopes into the house and hide them in the back of her closet. That night Andi came over, and they spent the evening in Debbie's bedroom, rolling the coins into paper sleeves to take to the bank. That took so long that Andi was forced to call home and ask permission to sleep over.

The mail load during the next two days was even heavier, and Bruce and Tim had to help with the coin rolling.

"If this is what it's like to work at a bank, it's no wonder Mr. Murdock's always in such a bad mood," Bruce grumbled.

Then the deluge began to lessen and, by the weekend, had subsided quite a bit. Even so, a couple dozen envelopes arrived on Saturday when Debbie's parents were home from work. They were understandably curious about the fact that their daughter was receiving more mail than they were, but when Debbie opened the envelopes at the breakfast table and they saw two quarters tumble out, they were more amused than perturbed.

"So your little business is a success!" Debbie's father said with a smile. "Congratulations, honey! It's nice that you and your friends are earning spending money in such a creative way."

Debbie nodded. That day's income equaled about twelve dollars. But her parents had no idea about the other envelopes that had been pouring in all week or about the many businesspeople who were purchasing space for ads for collars, leashes, sunglasses, earmuffs, mouthwash, and hand-knit sweaters for dogs.

By now there was more than enough in Bruce's bank account to cover the cost of Red Rover, and on Sunday afternoon he walked down the block to the Gordons' house to deliver his final payment.

Mr. Gordon regarded him with astonishment.

"Where did all this come from?" he asked, staring, dumbfounded, at the large pile of bills that Bruce had placed in his hand.

"Like I told you, I work for a newspaper," Bruce reminded him. "My sister and I and two of our friends are publishing it. Remember when I delivered a copy for Connor?"

"I do recall that, but I didn't realize —" Mr. Gordon seemed unable to find the words to complete his sentence. He kept staring at the money in amazement. "This is truly phenomenal. I'll go get Red Rover's papers for you. Those are important, as Red has an excellent pedigree. In the morning I'll have my secretary type up a bill of sale. I have to admit that I didn't really think you could do this. As I said, I'm extremely impressed. You're quite an entrepreneur!"

As soon as Mr. Gordon left the room, Jerry slid in through the half-open door to the patio. He apparently had been standing there listening to the entire conversation, and he looked like he'd just finished eating something that tasted bad.

"You can't have earned that much money selling newspapers," he said. "Connor and I haven't made that much with our subscriptions, and we've sold a lot of them."

"But, of course, you're donating half of what you make to charity," Bruce said. "By the way, what charity is it?"

"Don't try to change the subject," Jerry snapped. "I read Connor's copy of that paper, and it's junk. No one would want to pay to read your sister's dumb poems or that stupid gossip column. How are you making all that money? You must be doing something shady, and I'm going to find out what it is."

"Be my guest," Bruce said. "All we've done is publish a newspaper. Ever since we posted it on the Internet, we've been getting richer every day. People all over the country want to run ads. Now that I've paid for Red Rover, our bank account still has a balance of two hundred and seventy-six dollars. We're saving up now to buy cars."

Jerry opened his mouth to respond, but before he could do so, Mr. Gordon returned to the room with Red Rover's papers in his hand. He handed them over to Bruce with an expression of respect.

"I'm glad that you and Jerry have been chatting," he said. "You boys live right here on the same block, and it's a shame you're not better acquainted. Jerry, did you know that Bruce and his sister are publishing a newspaper? Maybe you'd like to apply for a job as a reporter."

"Bruce and I were just talking about his paper," Jerry said, gracing his father with one of his sweet smiles. "They have a pretty big staff already, but who knows? There may come a time when I can give them something they're looking for. If so, I'll be sure to let them know."

Bruce left the house with the feeling that something had slipped past him — that Jerry was referring to something that might be important — but he wasn't going to let himself worry about it. With Red's papers clutched in his hand, he broke into a run, charging through the gate into their backyard, where Red Rover was sitting dejectedly by his dog-house. As soon as he saw his master, he began to wag his tail, and his big brown eyes grew hopeful as he glanced toward the gate.

"You're not going to be cooped up here much longer," Bruce told him, throwing his arms around Red's neck and rubbing his cheek affectionately against the dog's silky head. "Tomorrow I get a bill of sale, and you're officially mine. Then we can go for runs all over the neighborhood."

When he broke the news to his parents, they regarded him with the same astonishment as Mr. Gordon.

"So, now do I get to take Red running?" Bruce asked his father.

"Oh, son, I don't know," Mr. Walker said, looking uncomfortable. "This situation really troubles me. That dog is so large and hard to control —"

"But, Dad, you *promised*!" Bruce cried. "You told me that when Red was legally mine I'd be able to take him running. Mom, you were there when he said it. You remember that, don't you?"

"You did tell him that," Mrs. Walker said to her husband. But she, too, looked distressed, as if she wished the promise hadn't been made.

"I acknowledge that promise," said Mr. Walker. "I meant it when I made it. But I never expected Bruce to buy the dog so quickly. I thought, by the time he managed to save up that much money, he'd have gone through a growth spurt. Red is a lot of dog for a boy his size to handle, especially if he decides to dash into the street again."

"He won't do that unless Jerry rams him," Bruce said. "And Jerry's not going to do that — not with his cousin, Connor, keeping a watch on him."

"Well, I'd like to be here to keep a watch on things, too," said Mr. Walker. "There's a problem I didn't anticipate when I made that promise. Your mother and I are going to be gone for three weeks. We're going to Europe to celebrate our fifteenth anniversary. We've been postponing telling you and Andi, because we knew that you wouldn't be happy about staying with Aunt Alice."

"We won't mind that at all," Bruce said. "I know you'll love Europe. Andi and I will be happy to stay with Aunt Alice."

If his parents had appeared startled when he'd told them he'd paid for Red Rover, that was nothing compared to the surprise on their faces now.

"Do you really mean that?" his mother asked

incredulously. "I've been so concerned! I've always dreamed of visiting Europe, and when your father surprised me with the tickets, I was so excited and happy I almost fainted. But I hated the thought of you children back here, miserable, and I'm worried about being out of reach in an emergency."

"There won't be an emergency," Bruce assured her. "And, if there is, Aunt Alice will know how to handle it. After all, she used to be a detective."

"That was a long time ago," his father said. "Aunt Alice is old now, and elderly people don't cope well with stressful situations. Your mother and I feel confident that Alice can deal with the ups and downs of everyday life, but we don't want her faced with a calamity. I want you to get a book about how to train dogs and teach Red to obey your commands. And I'm asking you to postpone taking him out of the yard until we're back from our trip. Then, if something goes wrong, we'll be here to help deal with it. Does that sound like a reasonable compromise?"

Bruce had to struggle to keep from showing his disappointment. He felt sure he could manage Red Rover without any difficulty, but he didn't want to ruin his parents' vacation by having them worry about him the whole time they were gone.

"Okay," he said. "I promise to wait till you get back."

The following evening he walked down to the Gordons' to collect the bill of sale. Mr. Gordon had it ready and complimented him again on his business initiative.

"It's wonderful to see young people so motivated," he said.

When Bruce left to go home, he found Connor in the Gordons' driveway, preparing to wax his car.

"Hi, dude, what's up?" Connor asked in his friendly manner. "Word has it you've got yourself a dog."

"Sure do!" Bruce said. "Now I'm going to start saving for a car. But I'll never be able to afford a set of wheels like yours. Someday, when you're not busy, would you take me for a ride?"

"I'd be glad to," Connor said, "but there isn't much time when I'm not busy, what with so much volunteer work and the job selling magazines."

"But I thought . . ." Bruce let the sentence trail off. Every time he talked to the Gordons he got more and more confused. It was as if their family never communicated and no one had any idea what the others were doing.

"What's with this *Dogs' Home Journal*?" he now asked Connor. "I can't seem to find it on the Internet."

"It's so new, the search engines haven't picked it up yet," Connor said. "And I have you to thank for finding it. I hadn't realized how popular dogs were in Elmwood. I figured you wouldn't mind if we added it to our subscription list. Business is business, and people who read a dog newspaper will read a dog magazine. Now that you're selling off the Internet, we're not in competition. No hard feelings, right, pal?"

He smiled his wonderful smile, and Bruce smiled back at him.

"No hard feelings," he said. "Like you say, it's all business."

Despite his resemblance to Jerry, it was impossible not to like Connor.

CHAPTER NINE

Now that Mr. and Mrs. Walker's trip was no longer a secret, it was suddenly all they could talk about. Bruce and Andi couldn't have imagined that a trip abroad took so much preparation. Their parents had to get passports, purchase new luggage, and buy voltage converters so they could take their hair dryer and electric razor. And there were endless discussions about what clothes they should pack, since parts of Europe were cold and others were hot.

"I just wish they'd leave and get it over with," Andi said irritably after what seemed like hours trapped at the family dinner table where their father had spread out maps and explained their travel routes and their mother had read aloud from an assortment of brochures.

Andi was so worn out by the demands of editing two newspapers that she had little energy to focus on anything else. Although the print edition of *The Bow-Wow News* was a weekly, they had decided to publish the Internet edition once every two weeks. To Andi's surprise, that required more work than the weekly. The second page of the online edition had to be sent individually to people who mailed them quarters, and typing all those e-mail addresses took forever.

There was also the challenge of having to select which lead article to feature on the Web site and exactly where to break it off so readers would be willing to pay to read the rest of it.

"Our second edition has to be about Barkley," Tim insisted. "Next to the issue about Bully, that one's our most popular."

"That picture doesn't look as clear as it did in the paper," Andi said, studying the image on the computer screen. "If Mr. Murdock says that's a stone, people might believe him."

"It is not a stone!" Bruce was outraged by the suggestion. "I know what it is! I was there when it happened!"

"But you weren't close enough," Andi said, continuing her critical examination of the photograph. "It actually *could* be a stone. Or maybe a dead bird."

"You can't have it both ways," Tim told her. "If

we use a picture that was taken from a far enough distance away so it shows both the dog and Mr. Murdock, the lump on the sidewalk won't show up in any detail. If we zero in on that, Bruce will have to crop out Mr. Murdock."

"I think I can fix that," Bruce said thoughtfully. "I can enlarge just that one little section of the picture. It won't be any harder than enlarging Bully's meat loaf."

"That would solve the problem," Andi said. "And I'll write a poem about it. I've already got the first verse:

The sidewalk glistened, clean and white,
Till Barkley ambled by.
His owner shouted, 'Hurry up!'
And hit him in the eye."

"You can't say that!" Bruce told her. "Mr. Murdock didn't hit Barkley in the eye!"

"*On the thigh!*" Andi hastily revised the verse. "That would rhyme. I'll change it. '*And hit him on the thigh!*'"

"He didn't hit him anywhere," Bruce said in exasperation. "All he did was yank his leash."

"That's almost as bad," Andi said. "He could have broken his neck. And 'leash' is hard to find a rhyme for. Debbie, how are you coming with the gossip column?"

"It's Bebe's turn to go to the Doggie Park," Debbie said, patting her mother's hair extensions into place. "And, instead of taking a notebook, I'm going to take a tape recorder. I don't want to miss a word when Fifi's owner tells Foxy's owner about her date with Dr. Bryant."

That week's gossip column was a long one. Not only did Dr. Bryant buy Fifi's owner dinner, he kissed her good night and gave her a handout about tick removal. In addition, Curly Roskin had eaten a pinecone, Frisky Mason had bitten the mail carrier, and Trixie Larkin had barked in the night and saved the family from a mouse that had gotten into the clothes hamper.

"I wouldn't feel safe if we didn't have Trixie," said Mrs. Larkin.

For the online edition, Andi decided to break off the article about Barkley at the point where it said, "Then the poor little dog lifted his trembling head and pleadingly gazed at his master as if to ask — FOR THE REST OF THIS HORRIFYING

STORY, SEND FIFTY CENTS AND YOUR E-MAIL ADDRESS TO *THE BOW-WOW NEWS*."

"What's 'the rest of the story'?" Bruce demanded. "Nothing more happened except Mr. Murdock yelled at me and I ran. When people send us money, what are you going to say Barkley was asking?"

"*'Dear Master, why don't you help Concerned Citizens for Clean Neighborhoods keep the sidewalks clean?'*" Andi said. "I know that's not worth fifty cents, but I'll send them my poem to make it longer. I did find a rhyme for 'leash.' It's 'quiche' — that awful cheese pie with broccoli that Aunt Alice makes.

His owner jerked
The sturdy leash
And yelled, 'Go home
And eat your quiche!' "

"You can't say Barkley ate quiche for breakfast," Bruce told her. "Not without a statement from the Murdocks. You're going to have to come up with a different poem."

The evening before Mr. and Mrs. Walker were due to leave, Aunt Alice invited the family over for dinner to discuss the details of the children's visit. Mr. Walker wanted to be sure that his aunt knew that Bruce was not to take Red Rover out of the yard, and Mrs. Walker wanted them all in agreement that the children would spend their evenings at home with Aunt Alice with no jaunts down the block to check on their dogs.

"Those dogs will do just fine on their own," she said. "I don't want you children out wandering around after dark."

Andi and Bruce had spent that afternoon at Tim's house, helping to print and assemble the next print edition of the paper. That had taken them longer than they'd expected, and when they finally arrived at Aunt Alice's house, their parents were already there. The three adults were in the living room with such somber expressions on their faces that the children knew immediately that something was wrong. Not just wrong, but *very* wrong. Mr. Walker was glowering, and Mrs. Walker looked as if she had been crying.

"Sit down," Mr. Walker said ominously. "We have something serious to discuss. I received a call at work today from Mr. Murdock. He is threatening to sue your mother and me as the guardians of minor children who have posted a libelous article and photo on the Internet. What have you and your friends done?"

"It wasn't libel," Andi said. "The story was true. Our legal advisor told us Mr. Murdock couldn't sue us."

"That's right," Aunt Alice interjected. "Andi consulted me about it. The facts of the story were documented by a photograph."

Mr. Walker regarded his aunt incredulously. "Are you saying you knew about this and didn't tell us?"

"It was a matter of confidentiality," Aunt Alice told him. "Andi asked my professional opinion, and I gave it to her. If the children had done something wrong, I would have felt obligated to say something, but they were within their rights. Mr. Murdock was the one who defied a town ordinance."

"I left a message on his answering machine," Bruce said. "When he didn't return the call, we figured his attorney told him he didn't have a case."

"That's not how things stand today," Mr. Walker

said. "Mr. Murdock's attorney believes he has grounds for a civil suit. Mr. Murdock says what you've posted on the Internet is completely different from what was in *The Bow-Wow News.* He says it's a total fabrication."

Bruce turned to Andi accusingly. "Did you post that poem about hitting Barkley in the eye?"

"No," Andi said. "I didn't even post about the quiche."

"I want to see what you've put on that Web site," Mr. Walker said. "Alice, I don't suppose you have a computer?"

"As a matter of fact, I do," Aunt Alice told him. "I've taken an interest in my old career again and I need to do online research."

She got up from the sofa and led the way up the stairs to what had been her sewing room. That room now looked very different. The sewing machine had been replaced with a computer and printer, and they were bracketed by bookshelves. The titles of the books all pertained to forensic science, police procedures, and criminal investigations.

"Some of those materials are outdated," Aunt

Alice said. "They've been stored for years in the attic, and while they've been gathering dust, the world has been changing all around us. I'm in the process of replacing them with books that I've ordered online. It's amazing how many investigative tools are available now that my husband and I never could have dreamed of."

She switched on the computer and the screen leapt to life. In a matter of seconds the current edition of *The Bow-Wow News* was there before them. The banner headline read "Barkley's Master Won't Scoop." Beneath that there was the picture of Barkley with Mr. Murdock.

"Oh, my!" Aunt Alice said softly. "I never imagined!"

Mr. Walker drew in a sharp breath and let it out slowly, as if he was afraid he might strangle on it.

"There's something wrong," Mrs. Walker said, staring at the image. "That pile on the sidewalk is *bigger than the dog!*"

"Maybe I enlarged it a little too much," Bruce conceded. "I wanted people to be able to tell what it was."

"You accomplished that," said Aunt Alice. "But, dear, there's so *much* of it! If Barkley produced something that size, the poor animal would be dead."

"This site must be closed down immediately!" Mr. Walker exploded. Bruce had never seen his father so angry. "Are you able to do that from here?"

"Tim can do it," Bruce said. "He's the one who set up the Web site. But this isn't Tim's fault. I took the photo and enhanced it."

"It's not Bruce's fault either," Andi said. "I gave him that assignment. If anybody goes to jail, it should be me."

"It doesn't matter whose idea it was," said Mr. Walker. "Parents are liable for the illegal actions of their children. And the timing couldn't be worse! Your mother and I are due to leave for Europe tomorrow."

"There's no way we can go," Mrs. Walker said in a whisper, struggling to hold back tears. "We can't possibly leave the country when all this legal activity is crashing down on us."

"Now, dear," Aunt Alice said gently, "this isn't as much of a catastrophe as you may imagine." She put a comforting arm around Mrs. Walker's shoulders. "I find it hard to believe there will be a lawsuit. If Mr. Murdock sues you, Concerned Citizens for Clean Neighborhoods will make posters and hold demonstrations. He doesn't want that sort of publicity. All he wants is for the article and the photo to go away."

"Phone Tim right now and tell him to take down the site," Mr. Walker told Bruce. "And if you have copies of that photo, destroy them."

"Yes, Bruce, do call Tim," said Aunt Alice. "My cell phone's there on my desk. But let's not be too hasty about destroying the photograph. You should probably destroy the enhancement, but let's keep the original. If Mr. Murdock makes problems for us in the future, we might need that photograph for evidence.

"Now, while Bruce is busy taking care of business, why don't the rest of us gather at the dinner table? By now, my quiche is probably all dried out."

CHAPTER TEN

Their parents did leave for Europe as scheduled, but not without a lot of agonizing. Mr. Walker spent much of the next morning on the phone with Mr. Murdock, while Mrs. Walker waited nervously by the open suitcases, uncertain whether she should continue packing or hang everything back in the closet.

When Mr. Walker finally announced that Mr. Murdock had agreed not to sue them, as long as the Web site was down and the children stopped publishing the newspaper, Mrs. Walker first sighed with relief and then announced, "We can't go."

"What do you mean, we can't go?" Mr. Walker said impatiently. "I told you, he's not going to sue."

"But what if something else happens while we're gone?" Mrs. Walker said.

"Everything will be fine," Aunt Alice assured her.

"I give you my word, the children won't publish another issue of *The Bow-Wow News*."

"But what about all the people who have taken out ads?" Andi asked. "And the people who paid three dollars for a summer subscription?"

"You will write them letters of apology and return their payments," her father told her firmly. "This is totally out of hand. How much money do you have in that bank account, anyway?"

"After I paid for Red Rover, it was two hundred and seventy-six dollars," Bruce said. "But now it's more, because we've gotten new ads and subscriptions."

"That's what I mean," wailed Mrs. Walker. "We can't leave now! There's so much that needs to be done to get all this straightened out!"

"I will see to that," Aunt Alice promised. "Now, hurry and go to the airport before you miss your plane."

So finally a taxi was summoned, and the suitcases were closed and loaded into the trunk. Then there were another ten minutes of hugs and kisses and a recitation of instructions. Andi was greatly relieved when the cab pulled out of the driveway and disappeared down the street, but even that wasn't the end of it. Their father phoned from the airport to make sure they understood that they were not to do anything — visit their friends, play with their dogs, write a poem, use the computer, watch TV — until all their financial obligations were dealt with.

But even with the Web site down, mail kept coming.

"Your letter carrier must be exhausted," Aunt Alice commented when Debbie arrived at her house with two plastic trash bags filled with envelopes.

"My parents won't let me bring these into our house," Debbie said. "Mr. Walker spooked them when he told them about Mr. Murdock's lawyer. They're afraid I'm going to be labeled a juvenile delinquent. They say this is ill-gotten money and we have to return it, but they don't want my finger-prints on it and they don't want my handwriting on the envelopes."

"You mean I'm going to have to answer these all by myself!" Andi exclaimed.

"The four of you must do it together," said Aunt Alice. "After all, this business was a partnership. Debbie can wear my garden gloves so she won't leave prints, and she can print the addresses in block letters. And there's no way that any of you are juvenile delinquents. You just tried to do too much and made a few small mistakes."

Although they did work together writing notes and addressing envelopes, there wasn't much conversation. Tim was angry about having to take down the Web site, and Debbie was heartsick that her new gossip column would go unpublished. For their part, Bruce and Andi were upset that the hours of laborious paperwork were forcing them to neglect their dogs.

By the third day, however, the money had been returned, and they were reunited with their pets. Although Bruce couldn't take Red running, he did buy a book about dog training and spent many hours teaching him to respond to commands. Andi and Debbie took Bebe and Friday to the Doggie Park, where Friday huddled next to Andi's ankles, but Bebe had a fine time. Debbie took along her tape recorder, even though she wasn't writing her column anymore.

"It's gotten to be a habit," she told Andi. "Like Bruce with his photography, I've found my life's calling — I was placed on this earth to be a spy. The odd thing is that there seems to be so few dogs here. Trixie and Foxy and Fifi aren't anywhere around."

Mr. and Mrs. Walker phoned often from Europe and sent e-mail from Internet cafés. After the first few days, when they worried constantly about what was going on back in Elmwood, they seemed to start to relax and really have fun.

Aunt Alice continued to assure them that everything was fine, although that wasn't exactly true. Andi was dusting the living room furniture, which was one of the chores she had to do each day, when Aunt Alice arrived home from her weekly Garden Club meeting. Normally she returned from those meetings bubbling with enthusiasm, loaded down with packets of seeds and clippings from plants. Today she should have been especially happy because she was carrying an armful of roses with bright pink centers and white petals. But she seemed more worried than delighted.

"After the meeting, I talked with Mrs. Bernstein," she told Andi. "She's distressed about what seems to have happened to a recipe that she gave to *The Bow-Wow News*. She says her friends who went online and ordered it are no longer talking to her.

Did you mail out something different from what was in the paper?"

"I did change a few things," Andi admitted. "A veterinarian told us that some of the ingredients in Bully's favorite meat loaf weren't good for dogs, so I replaced those with things that are healthier."

"Like dog food?" Aunt Alice speculated.

"Only the best," Andi assured her. "The man who makes that dog food was one of our advertisers."

"Well, that explains it," Aunt Alice said. "All the Bernsteins' friends who have eaten at their home have told them they're not coming back. They must think the meat loaf she served them was made with dog food."

"Oh, no!" Andi exclaimed. "Poor Mrs. Bernstein! I'll call her right now and apologize."

She rushed to the phone and dialed the Bernsteins' number. Mr. Bernstein answered immediately.

"Yes?" he said. His voice sounded strained and unnatural. For a moment Andi wasn't even sure who he was.

"This is Andi Walker," she said. "Is Mrs. Bernstein there, please?"

"She can't come to the phone," Mr. Bernstein said. "We don't want to tie up the line. Can I give her a message?"

"Please tell her I'm sorry about the meat loaf recipe," Andi said. "I didn't mean to make her friends mad at her. I'd print a retraction, except we no longer have the newspaper, but if she'd like for me to write personal letters to the people who ordered the recipe —"

"Forget it," Mr. Bernstein said shortly. "We have far worse things to worry about. I'm going to have to hang up now. Please don't call back. We need to keep our line open for a very important call."

There was a sharp click as he hung up.

Andi felt a chill of apprehension. Something dreadful had happened to the Bernsteins, and it didn't seem likely it had anything to do with Mr. Murdock.

Bruce was at their house, putting Red Rover through a training session, so Andi raced down the block and burst in through the backyard gate.

"We need to go to the Bernsteins' right now!" she told him.

"Why? What's happened?" Bruce asked her.

"Aunt Alice saw Mrs. Bernstein at Garden Club," Andi said. "The friends who ordered our meat loaf recipe think she served it to *them*. When I called to apologize, Mr. Bernstein wouldn't let me talk to her. He said he was waiting for an important call and hung up on me. I'm afraid Mrs. Bernstein may have eaten the wrong meat loaf. Maybe the dog food made her sick, and Mr. Bernstein is waiting for a call from the doctor."

"If Mrs. Bernstein was sick, she wouldn't have been at Garden Club," Bruce said reasonably. "It sounds like something's wrong, but it can't be that."

"You're right," Andi agreed, relaxing a little. "Still, I think we ought to go over there. Maybe Mr. Bernstein is the one who's sick, and that's why he sounded so funny. Or maybe Mrs. Bernstein is so upset about the meat loaf that she's locked herself in the bathroom."

"That's ridiculous," Bruce said. "But, yes, of course we should go over there. Whatever's wrong, we want to do what we can to help them."

When they arrived at the Bernsteins' house, a pile of white roses was lying on the front steps as if somebody had thrown them down in a frenzy.

"Mrs. Bernstein got those at Garden Club," Andi said. "Aunt Alice came home with some just like them. But why did Mrs. Bernstein drop hers on the steps?"

She bent to gather up the scattered blossoms while Bruce pressed the doorbell. He waited a couple of minutes and, when nobody came to the door, pressed it again.

"Maybe they're not home," he said after more minutes went by without a response.

"Somebody is," Andi said. "I saw the curtain in the dining room window move. Someone was peeking out."

Bruce rang the bell a third time. This time the doorknob rattled and the door was pulled open several inches. Mrs. Bernstein's voice asked fearfully, "Who is it?"

"It's just us, Bruce and Andi," Bruce said. "We got worried when Mr. Bernstein said you couldn't come to the phone. We wanted to check and make sure that you're okay."

The door was opened a bit farther, and Mrs. Bernstein peeked through the crack.

"It *is* you!" she exclaimed. "I thought so when I looked out the window, but I had to be certain. People sometimes disguise themselves, especially criminals." She opened the door all the way and motioned them inside. "It's all right, dear," she called to her husband. "It's the Walker children."

Mr. Bernstein stepped out suddenly from behind the door. He was gripping a baseball bat and looked as if he was getting ready to swing at a high-flying ball. He lowered it with a sigh of relief.

"I'm glad I didn't have to use this thing," he said. "I'm a peaceful man, but I would have done it if I had to. People do what they must to protect their own."

"What's been happening here?" Bruce asked anxiously, as Mrs. Bernstein closed and locked the front door. She still hadn't reached to take the flowers from Andi's hands. It was as if she didn't even see them.

"Bully has been dognapped," she said.

"Dognapped!" Bruce exclaimed. "You mean somebody stole him?"

"It's my fault," Mr. Bernstein cried in an agonized voice. "I shouldn't have left him unguarded. I was his guardian and protector while my wife was at her meeting. I failed our Bully, and I'll never forgive myself."

"Tell us what happened," Andi said softly. She had never seen a grown man so close to tears before.

"Bully was in the backyard, playing in his sandbox," said Mr. Bernstein. "I was with him, of course, helping him build a sand castle. Then I heard the phone ring. I left him for just a minute to run inside and answer it. It was my wife, calling on her cell phone. She was going to stop at the grocery store and wanted to know what flavor ice cream to get. I told her, 'chocolate raspberry ripple with almonds.' Then I rushed back outside, and the gate was open. Bully was gone."

"Maybe the gate wasn't tightly latched," Bruce suggested. "Maybe it just swung open all on its own, and Bully ran out. If we form a search party and cover the neighborhood, we'll find him."

"That was our first thought, too," Mrs. Bernstein said. "When I got home, Mr. Bernstein came rushing out to meet me. He told me what happened, and I dropped those flowers on the steps and raced straight through the house and out into the backyard. It was just as he told me, the gate was standing open. But there was something else — a note in the sandbox, stuck like a flag, right on top of Bully's dear castle. It was a ransom note demanding two hundred dollars."

"It's my fault," Mr. Bernstein said again, his face buried in his hands. "Why did I have to tell you 'chocolate raspberry ripple with almonds'? If I'd just said, 'vanilla,' I'd have gotten back to Bully sooner. Those extra few seconds might have made all the difference."

"May Andi and I see the ransom note?" Bruce asked them.

"We can't show that to anyone," Mrs. Bernstein told him. "The dognapper said if we went to the police or showed that note to anybody, Bully would suffer. He told us to put two hundred dollars in a book called *Old Yeller* at the Elmwood library. Mr. Bernstein just got back from doing that. When you rang the doorbell we didn't know what to think. We prayed it was somebody bringing Bully home, but we knew in our hearts that it was much too soon for that. So then we thought the dog-napper might have come back to demand some other form of ransom. If he could take our Bully, that terrible person could do anything!"

"If we can't go to the police, then what can we do?" Bruce asked.

"Nothing," Mr. Bernstein said helplessly. "All we can do is sit by the phone and wait."

CHAPTER ELEVEN

The hardest part was feeling so helpless. Although Bruce and Andi wanted desperately to stay with the Bernsteins, they had to go back to Aunt Alice's house for dinner. Not only that, but they had to stay there all evening, as they'd promised their parents they wouldn't leave the house after dinner.

To make matters worse, they couldn't even phone the Bernsteins. That would tie up their line and make it impossible for the dognapper to contact them.

So they dutifully ate their chicken and their spinach salad and responded to Aunt Alice's questions about what they had done that day and whether they had read their parents' e-mail from Paris and did they think the white roses would look better in the blue vase or the crystal one.

"Would you like to start coming to Garden Club with me?" she asked Andi. "It's never too early to start learning about flower arranging."

"Maybe sometime," Andi said, trying not to seem ungracious. "It does sound interesting, but I'm kind of busy right now."

Aunt Alice regarded her with surprise. "What are you doing now that you're no longer publishing a newspaper?"

"I'm writing a novel," Andi told her. The words leapt out of her mouth of their own volition, but as soon as she heard herself say them, she knew they were true. She was going to write a novel, and she would start it immediately. Like her poems, that novel was probably already inside her, just waiting for her to pick up a pencil and release it.

"What is your novel about?" Aunt Alice asked with interest.

"About a dog," Andi said immediately. "He vanishes from his yard, and his owners are afraid he's been dognapped. They're so scared of the dognapper that they start carrying baseball bats in case the criminal comes back to do something even worse."

Bruce glared at her across the table and silently mouthed, *"Shut up!"*

Luckily, Aunt Alice didn't see him.

"That sounds like an exciting story," she said. "I hope it has a happy ending."

"So do I," Andi said fervently.

In the kitchen after dinner, as Bruce scraped plates and Andi loaded the dishwasher, he hissed at her, "You *told*! You promised you wouldn't, and you did! You told her about Bully!"

"I did not," Andi hissed back. "I told her about a book I'm going to write. I can't help it if the plot is like something that's really happened. All good plots are realistic."

"Novels are *fiction*," Bruce said. "If you put true stuff in there — one single name or detail about a real person — it won't be just Mr. Murdock's lawyer who'll come after you. Every real person that you put in that book will have a lawyer."

Since Bruce was too angry to talk to her, and she was afraid that if she stayed downstairs Aunt Alice would ask her to help arrange roses, Andi went up to the guest room, which was her bedroom while she was staying there, and got out a notebook and pencil.

She opened the notebook and sat for a moment, enjoying the empty page. The pure white paper with thin blue lines running across it, waiting to be covered with words, made her very happy. She realized that wasn't the way most people felt about notebooks. In fact, she had never met anyone who admitted to feeling that way, although, of course, she didn't go around asking people. But somewhere out there, there must be others like herself, hiding in their bedrooms, admiring empty pages, too afraid of being considered "weird" to admit to the joy they were feeling. She hoped that when she grew up she would marry such a person.

Chapter One, she wrote.

That was the easy part. She knew how the story should start, but she also knew that Bruce was right, a novel was supposed to be fiction. She would have to change names and details to conceal identities.

Bobby, the old basset hound, sat by the high iron wall. The next-door neighbors built that wall because they didn't want Bobby to see his sweetheart, Juliet. Juliet was ravishingly beautiful. She was a

Andi paused to consider what Juliet should be. She couldn't make her an Airedale, because that would be too much like Ginger. She considered making her a greyhound, since greyhounds had springy legs and could jump over walls, but it was hard to imagine Bobby falling in love with a dog with such a strangely shaped body. She decided to make Juliet a poodle. Then she could fashion her looks on Snowflake Swanson.

She was a poodle. She was very exotic and won a lot of beauty contests. Every week her owners took her to have her toenails painted. Now, as he sat in his yard, Bobby could hear her on the other side of the wall, making little whining sounds. He pictured her glamorous purple toenails. He made little whining sounds back.

Andi paused again. How could she get the lovers together if Juliet couldn't jump the wall? Bobby the Basset certainly couldn't do it, especially since she'd made him old. The only way to get Bobby out of his yard was through the back gate like the real Bully Bernstein. Bruce had suggested that the Bernsteins' gate might have swung open accidentally. That seemed as good a solution as any.

Bobby glanced at the gate, and he couldn't believe his good fortune. His master had forgotten to close the latch when he took out the garbage. Bobby rushed to the gate and shoved it open. In an instant he was galloping down the alley to the gate to Juliet's yard. Sad to say, that gate was latched. Bobby made a whining sound. Juliet raced right over and started hurling her slender body against the gate with all her might. Bobby jumped against it from his side. Maybe, between the two of them, they could knock that gate down!

Then, all of a sudden, Bobby heard a thunderous voice. It was Juliet's owner, Mr. Rinkle. "What the devil do you think you're doing?" he shouted. He threw the gate open and grabbed Bobby and yanked him inside. "This will teach your owners to keep their gate shut!" he bellowed. He hauled Bobby over to the toolshed and shoved him in on top of the lawn mower. "Ha, ha, ha!" He laughed wickedly.

Andi reviewed the words she had written. She was pleased with the story so far, but what should she write next? It was in character for somebody as cruel as Mr. Rinkle to want to punish Bobby's owners by giving them a scare. But, after shutting the dog in the toolshed, what would he do? He couldn't keep him there forever.

The answer leapt into her mind as if somebody was dictating it: *Mr. Rinkle would ask Bobby's owners for ransom!*

Andi dropped the notebook onto her bed and raced down to the den, where Bruce was watching television.

"Where's Aunt Alice?" she asked him.

"Gone to bingo," Bruce said.

"I know what happened to Bully!" Andi announced excitedly. "The Tinkles dognapped him!"

"Give me a break!" Bruce said. "I don't like Mr. Tinkle any more than you do, but he wouldn't do that."

"How do you know?" Andi demanded. "You know how the Tinkles hate Bully and how mad they get at the thought of his being with Ginger. What if Bully's gate swung open, just like you thought? Wouldn't he rush down the alley and go straight to Ginger? What if he managed to get into the yard, and Mr. Rinkle — I mean, Mr. Tinkle — caught the two dogs together? What if he realized Ginger was still in love with Bully? What if he got so mad that he locked Bully in their toolshed?"

"Do the Tinkles have a toolshed?" Bruce was beginning to become intrigued despite himself.

"If they don't, they must have someplace else they could put him," Andi said. "Like a storage closet in the garage."

"But what about the ransom note?" Bruce asked. "If Bully got out of his yard on his own, how would the ransom note have gotten stuck in the sand castle?"

"After he locked Bully up, Mr. Tinkle went in through the Bernsteins' back gate and planted the note," Andi said, continuing the story. "Nobody was there to see him. Mr. Bernstein was inside on the phone with Mrs. Bernstein."

"Why would Mr. Tinkle do that?" Bruce asked skeptically. "The Tinkles have plenty of money. They don't need two hundred dollars."

"He didn't do it for the money," Andi said. "He wanted to punish the Bernsteins for letting Bully run loose. Mr. Tinkle probably won't even pick up the ransom. In the morning he'll let Bully back out into the alley, and Bully will run home. Mr. Tinkle will have gotten his revenge, and Bully will never visit Ginger again."

"It's possible it might have happened that way," Bruce conceded. "If so, we can't let the Bernsteins spend the whole night worrying. We've got to find out if Bully is in the toolshed."

"I could call Tiffany," Andi said.

"As if she would tell you!"

"I could tell her we already know because a tip-ster called us," Andi said. "I could say I'm calling to warn her that the police are on their way and she needs to get Bully back to the Bernsteins immediately."

"I don't suppose there's anything to lose," Bruce said. "If the Tinkles *aren't* guilty, the worst they can do is laugh at you."

"And if they *are* guilty, they'll set Bully free," Andi said. "Can't you picture the Bernsteins' faces when Bully comes racing in through his dog door! I wish we could be there to see it!"

"Okay, I'm with you," Bruce said. "Go ahead and call Tiffany."

Andi dialed the Tinkles' number, hoping against hope that it would be Tiffany who answered and not her father.

It turned out to be neither. It was Mrs. Tinkle.

"Who are you and what do you want?" she demanded.

Andi was taken aback by the abruptness of the question.

"I'm a friend of Tiffany's," she said, "or, at least, I used to be. May I speak to her, please?"

"Tiffany can't come to the phone," said Mrs. Tinkle. "What are you calling her about?"

Now that she was faced with the question, Andi discovered that she didn't have the nerve to tell a complete lie. If she'd been talking to Tiffany, she might have been able to, but not to Mrs. Tinkle.

"I just wondered if Ginger's had any visitors lately," she said lamely.

She was not prepared for the resounding shriek that followed.

"What do you know about Ginger's visitors?" Mrs. Tinkle screamed. "What have you done with Ginger?"

"Nothing," Andi said shakily. "I haven't seen Ginger in months. I was just calling to see if Bully Bernstein was over there and maybe ended up in your toolshed. By accident, of course."

But Mrs. Tinkle was too hysterical to respond to her. Then, apparently, the receiver was snatched from her hand and a man's voice shouted, "What do you want from us now? I left the money in the *Howliday Inn* book two hours ago. Why isn't Ginger back yet?"

Andi hastily hung up.

"I got Mrs. Tinkle," she said.

"I guessed that much," Bruce said. "I could hear her screaming all the way across the room. Then I heard Mr. Tinkle yelling, too, but I couldn't make out what they were saying."

"I think Ginger's been dognapped," Andi said. "The Tinkles thought I was the dognapper. Mr. Tinkle said he put the money in the *Howliday Inn* book. That's a book about dogs, and so is *Old Yeller*. I've read both of them. Bruce, this is getting crazy. What's going on?"

"Obviously Mr. Tinkle is innocent," Bruce said. "There's a dognapper loose in Elmwood. He's taken two dogs that we know of, and who knows how many others? Maybe dozens!"

"Maybe hundreds!" Andi said. "When Debbie and I were at the Doggie Park, there were hardly any dogs there. Trixie used to go there all the time, and so did Fifi and Curly and Frisky and all the other dogs Debbie wrote about in her gossip column. But they weren't there yesterday. Debbie couldn't understand it."

"Maybe the owners caught on to where Debbie was getting her gossip," Bruce suggested. But Andi could tell by his voice that he didn't believe that. He was just trying to make her feel better.

"I'm going to phone the Larkins," she said. "Mrs. Larkin loved our story about 'Trixie the Hero Dog.' I know she'll be willing to talk to me."

When she dialed the Larkins' number, Mrs. Larkin answered immediately, just as Mrs. Tinkle had.

"It's Andi Walker," Andi said quickly so as not to alarm her. "I'm not calling with information or anything. I just got thinking about Trixie and was wondering how she was."

"Trixie is — away from home — right now," Mrs. Larkin said nervously. "We're hoping she'll be back soon."

Andi said, "Mrs. Larkin, I hate to ask you this, but is it possible Trixie's been dognapped?"

Mrs. Larkin started to cry.

"You mustn't tell anyone," she sobbed. "The ransom note said that if we tell, something terrible will happen to Trixie."

"Did the dognapper tell you to leave money in a book?" Andi asked her.

Mrs. Larkin sounded startled by the question. "How did you know?"

"It's what dognappers do," Andi said. "And the books are often about dogs."

"*Where the Red Fern Grows*," said Mrs. Larkin. "At the Elmwood library. I had to get the money from an ATM machine, so I didn't get to the library until just as it was closing. That means we can't possibly get Trixie back tonight. I'm not going to sleep a wink, knowing Trixie's not here to protect us."

"Don't you think you should call the police?" Andi asked her.

"No!" Mrs. Larkin cried frantically. "We can't risk endangering Trixie. We're not a well-to-do family, but money means nothing compared to Trixie! Promise you won't call the police!"

"I promise," Andi said. "I'm going to hang up now so you can keep your line open. I'll call you tomorrow to see if Trixie's back, which I'm certain she will be."

But she wasn't certain at all.

When she hung up the phone, Bruce said, "Well, that makes the third one. I don't want to call Mr. Murdock, but I guess I'll have to. If Barkley's gone, he'll try to blame that on us."

He dialed the Murdocks' number, listened, and hung up.

"What happened?" Andi asked. "Did you get the answering machine?"

"No," Bruce said. "I got Mr. Murdock in person, and I couldn't think of what to say to him. The good news is, Barkley hasn't been dognapped. I could hear him yapping in the background. It's your turn now. We need to check on Snowflake."

Mrs. Swanson seemed delighted to hear from Andi and wasn't at all opposed to tying up the line.

"Snowflake was in another beauty contest today," she said. "She only got honorable mention, which was a bit of a letdown, but, of course, the poor thing is getting older. Youth means so much in show business. Please, don't mention that in your newspaper. We wouldn't want people to think that Snowflake's a has-been."

"We won't put a thing in *The Bow-Wow News*," Andi assured her. It was the easiest promise she'd ever made.

"Snowflake is safe," she told Bruce when she hung up the phone. "What can we do now? We've promised we won't call the police, but we've got to find some way to stop this."

"Mrs. Larkin said she delivered the ransom to the library at closing time," Bruce said. "That means the dognapper hasn't had a chance to pick it up yet. One of us needs to be at the library as soon as it opens and keep an eye on that book. Whoever picks up that money is going to be the dognapper."

"You and I can do that together," Andi said eagerly.

"I wish we could," Bruce told her, "but we're too well-known. The missing dogs — at least, the ones we're aware of — all were featured in *The Bow-Wow News*. It's possible that's why the dognappers chose them to dognap — our newspaper made them famous. You and I might be recognized if we stake out the library. Much as I hate to give this assignment to a ding-a-ling, I'm afraid it's got to be Debbie. Nobody knows what she looks like because she wears disguises."

CHAPTER TWELVE

Debbie didn't return from the library until late in the morning. The others had been at the Walker house, waiting for her to turn up, ever since the library opened. Andi was on the sofa in the den, reading to Bebe and Friday. Tim and MacTavish were sprawled on the carpet, and Tim was restlessly surfing TV channels.

Bruce had spent most of the morning in the backyard, working off nervous energy by tussling with Red Rover. Now he came into the house to check the wall clock to make sure that his watch hadn't stopped. It didn't seem possible that time could be passing so slowly. Bruce was not accustomed to inactivity, and it was almost more than he could bear to have Debbie out solving the mystery while the rest of them just sat there.

"What do you bet she forgot to go?" Bruce said. "Maybe she's at home, reading a magazine."

"She wouldn't do that," Andi said. "I'm sure she's at the library. Maybe she's late because she's made a citizen's arrest and captured the dognapper herself."

When Debbie finally did arrive, Andi jumped to her feet so quickly that Bebe and Friday went tumbling into the hollow that she had left in the sofa cushion. Debbie was wearing the disguise she used when she went out with MacTavish — black jeans, black T-shirt, black baseball cap. Bruce thought she looked like a character in a cartoon. But MacTavish leapt up from the rug and rushed to greet her. He apparently expected to be taken to the Doggie Park.

"So what happened?" Tim asked Debbie.

"Nothing," she said. "The dognapper didn't come."

"Why didn't you stay and wait for him?" Bruce demanded. "Your assignment was to hang out there until you saw who picked up the money."

"I stayed as long as I needed to," Debbie said. "I was the first person there when the library opened. I went straight to the children's book room and found *Where the Red Fern Grows* and sat down in a chair across from it. A day-care group came in to have their story hour, and I learned all about trolls and ogres and wicked stepmothers."

"So why did you leave?" Bruce asked her. "Did you just get bored?"

"I completed the mission," Debbie said. "When story hour was over, I waited another ten minutes to see if anybody came for the ransom. Then I went over and pulled that book off the shelf. There was nothing in it. I looked at the other two books people told us they left ransom in. There wasn't any money in them, either. The dognapper must have gotten it before I got there."

"That doesn't seem possible," Bruce said. "He might have collected the money from those other books, but not from *Where the Red Fern Grows*. Mrs. Larkin left it just as the library was closing, and you got there this morning when it opened."

"Maybe the dognapper is a librarian," Tim suggested.

"No way!" Andi said firmly. "No librarian would do anything illegal. They don't even bend down corners of books to mark their places."

"Something odd did happen while I was there," Debbie said. "From where I was sitting in the children's room, I could see out into the main library. I think I saw Mr. Bernstein come in the front door and go over to the adult section."

"You *think* you saw him, or you really *did* see him?" Bruce asked her. "You know Mr. Bernstein. Why didn't you go over and speak to him?"

"I didn't get a good look at him," Debbie said defensively. "Besides, I was in disguise, and it was right in the middle of story hour. I'd have had to get up and shove my way through all those little kids. And what if it wasn't Mr. Bernstein? I'd have blown my cover for nothing."

"If the ransom money for Bully and Ginger was collected, then maybe those dogs have been returned to their owners," Bruce said. "I'm going to call the Bernsteins."

It was Mr. Bernstein who answered.

"It's Bruce," Bruce told him. "I just wanted to know if Bully's back."

"No," Mr. Bernstein said. "And things have gotten worse. The dognapper's demanded more money. This morning he asked for another two hundred dollars."

"Did he call you?" Bruce asked him eagerly. "Did you hear his voice? Could you tell anything about him?"

"He didn't phone," Mr. Bernstein said. "He left another note. He stuck it through the mail slot in our front door at some point during the night. It was there when my wife and I woke up this morning — not that we'd ever really slept. We lay awake most of the night. Every time we heard any kind of sound, like a branch brushing against a window, we hoped it might be the dognapper bringing Bully back. But we were too afraid to get up and check, in case we caught him in the act and he got violent. I'm not good enough with a baseball bat to protect us. In fact, I never played baseball, even as a kid. That bat belonged to our son. I sometimes pick it up and hold it, just because he used to hold it. I like to think I feel the touch of his fingers on the handle."

"So you left more ransom," Bruce said. He already knew the answer.

"Our Social Security checks came yesterday," Mr. Bernstein said. "So we had enough money to do that. I took it to the library this morning and left it in a book. This time it was *The Incredible Journey* in the adult section. I know you must think we're fools for giving in to blackmail, but this second note was worse than the first one. It threatened horrible things if we didn't pay."

His voice was shaking so badly that he could barely speak.

"That's all right," Bruce said hastily. "I'd have done the same thing."

"Thank you," Mr. Bernstein said. "You're a kind young man. It's hard for most people to understand what Bully means to us. You see, our only child — the boy who played baseball — was killed in a car wreck. We were too old to have more children, and we wouldn't have done that anyway — you can't replace one beloved child with another. But eventually we did get a dog and, for my wife in particular, Bully has been a source of comfort. She can pour out some of the love she has stored up inside her onto a sweet, gentle animal who loves her back. I hope you can understand and don't think we're too foolish."

"I don't think that at all," Bruce told him. "I think you're both very brave. I promise we'll get Bully back. My sister and I and our friends won't rest until we find him."

He hung up the phone and sat there, staring at the wall. He had made an impulsive promise based solely on emotion, and how in the world could he keep it? Debbie's efforts at spying had not accomplished anything other than to further confuse them.

"What about fingerprints?" Tim suggested. "There must be prints on the ransom notes."

"We don't know how to lift fingerprints," Bruce reminded him. "And even if we did, what would we do with them? None of the victims will let us report the dognappings."

"Maybe we ought to call in Aunt Alice," said Andi.

"She'd go straight to the police," Tim said. "All adults would do that unless they owned one of the hostages."

"Not Aunt Alice," Andi said. "We can tell things to her in confidence. She didn't tell our parents about Mr. Murdock. And even though she's been retired for a long time, she's getting back into detective work."

"She probably would be willing to help us," Bruce agreed. "But I don't think she'd know how to do it. She isn't up on new technology."

"I'll go back to the library and keep a watch on *The Incredible Journey*," Debbie said. "If Mr. Bernstein left money this morning, it may still be there."

"I'll go with you," Tim said. "This requires two people — one to keep an eye on the book, and the other to watch for the Tinkles. If they got a second ransom note like the Bernsteins, one of them is sure to come in with more money."

"That's a good plan," Bruce said. "And while the two of you stake out the library, Andi and I will go over to the Larkins'. We need to know whether they've been asked for more ransom."

"Just give me a minute to get Bebe and Friday their lunch," Andi said. "While I'm at it, does anyone else want a tuna sandwich?"

"You're going to make those dogs tuna sandwiches?" Bruce exclaimed. "Don't you remember the e-mail from the veterinarian?"

"I'll leave out the lettuce and cut the crusts off the bread," Andi said. "And I won't use very much mayonnaise."

Bruce shook his head in disgust. "Okay, while you're poisoning your dogs, I'll go refill Red's water bowl. Let's meet back here at five. Then Andi and I can get back to Aunt Alice's by dinnertime."

He went out to the kitchen, gathered up a handful of biscuits, and let himself out the back door to get Red's water bowl.

The back gate was standing open.

So, Red's gone running, Bruce thought. *He's given up on me and decided to stretch his legs on his own.*

But how could the gate have swung open all by itself? He could see no way that it could have come unlatched, since he and Andi had entered the house through the front door and he had gone out to the backyard through the kitchen. Neither of them had touched the gate.

"Red!" he called with desperation in his voice. "Red, *come!*"

But he already knew that shouting for Red would be futile — that no big dog would come streaking in through that gate — because by now he had seen the sheet of paper posted on Red's doghouse.

His instinct was to snatch it off, but he managed to control himself and carefully peel the note off the roof with his fingernails, touching only the edges in order to preserve fingerprints.

The message was printed in block letters:

IF YOU EVER WANT TO SEE YOUR DOG ALIVE AGAIN, LEAVE $276 IN A COPY OF <u>LASSIE COME HOME</u> IN THE ELMWOOD LIBRARY. IF YOU SHOW

THIS NOTE TO ANYONE OR GO TO THE POLICE, YOUR DOG WILL SUFFER A FATE WORSE THAN DEATH.

He heard the kitchen door open and then slam shut as Andi came out of the house.

"Bebe and Friday are enjoying their lunch," she said. "Are you ready to go to the Larkins'?" When Bruce didn't answer, she crossed the yard to stand beside him. "Bruce, what is it?" she cried when she saw her brother's face. "You look like you're going to be sick!"

"Red's been dognapped," Bruce told her. "It's just like the others, except that this time it's *Red*! It happened while we were only feet away in the den! We were sitting there, talking about dognappings and feeling so sorry for the Bernsteins and Larkins, and I wasn't giving a single thought to my *own* dog!"

"Let's call the police," Andi said. "We can do that without breaking promises if all we report is Red."

"Are you crazy?" Bruce exclaimed. "I'm not going to risk Red Rover. What we need is a private investigator. *We need Aunt Alice.*"

CHAPTER THIRTEEN

"Calm down, Bruce," Aunt Alice said. "I understand how upset you are, but it's not going to help Red Rover to have his master fall to pieces. We must keep our wits about us and sort through the information."

"I already gave you all the information," Bruce said.

Actually, he had given her half of it and had then become so emotional that he couldn't go on. When he first realized Red was missing, Bruce had gone into a state of shock. An unnatural calm descended upon him, as if he were cushioned in cotton, and all his natural reflexes had closed down. But here, in Aunt Alice's living room, as he relived that terrible moment when he noticed the gate standing open and then spotted the note on the doghouse, his knees had gotten weak and his voice had cracked so badly that he couldn't continue.

So Andi had taken up the story and filled in the pieces about Bully and Ginger and Trixie and all the other dogs from the Doggie Park who had been mentioned in Debbie's gossip column and now were missing.

"I'd like to see the ransom note," said Aunt Alice.

"I've got it here," Bruce told her. "I haven't touched it except by the edges."

"Good thinking," Aunt Alice said approvingly. "Andi, go get a Ziploc bag. We have to protect this note. The time may come when we'll need to have it dusted for fingerprints."

"You promised you wouldn't go to the police!" Bruce protested.

"I won't," Aunt Alice assured him. "Not without your permission, because you're my client. But I need you to be calm and objective. There are clues — there are *always* clues — and you're going to have to help me find them. Here comes Andi; let's get that note into the freezer bag and then try to analyze it."

Once the note was securely encased, Aunt Alice read it carefully.

"Is there anything here that strikes you as odd?" she asked Bruce.

"It's the same as the other notes," he said. "The families told us what was in those. They were to leave the ransom money in books at the library, and all those books were about dogs."

"The amount the dognapper is asking for seems unusual," Aunt Alice said. "Two hundred and seventy-six dollars. Is that the same amount he demanded for the other dogs?"

"No," Andi said. "He asked two hundred dollars for the others. Then, when the Bernsteins paid it, he asked for two hundred more."

"So, why would he demand this particular amount from you?" Aunt Alice asked. "Is there any significance in that?"

"It's the amount I told Dad that we had in our account," Bruce said, beginning to follow her thinking.

"Who else was aware of that amount?" asked Aunt Alice.

"Mr. Murdock may know," Andi said. "He's vice president of the bank."

"Mr. Murdock," Aunt Alice repeated thoughtfully. "That's an interesting suggestion. Do you happen to know if Barkley is among the hostages?"

"He's not," Bruce said. "I phoned the Murdocks and heard him barking."

"Snowflake wasn't dognapped either," Andi said. "But I'm sure Mrs. Swanson is innocent. All she's interested in is having Snowflake win contests."

"Mr. Murdock doesn't fit the profile either," said Aunt Alice. "It's very unlikely a banker would be a dognapper. He wouldn't want dog hair on his suit. I want both of you to concentrate. Try to recall if you've ever mentioned to anyone other than your parents the exact amount you had in the bank."

"Not me," Andi said. "I didn't even know how much it was. Bruce, Tim, and Debbie took care of the finances."

"How about you, Bruce?" Aunt Alice asked. "Is it possible there was a time when you divulged that information?"

"I might have told Jerry," Bruce said. "He called our paper stupid, and I got so mad that I bragged about how successful we were. I actually may have told him the amount in the bank."

"Jerry!" Aunt Alice said. "My, isn't that interesting!"

"I don't think it's Jerry," Bruce said. "Connor wouldn't allow it. He watches over Jerry like a hawk."

"Do you mean those two boys spend every second together?" asked Aunt Alice.

"Well, no," Bruce said. "Connor does spend time on volunteer work. It's possible Jerry's involved in stuff Connor doesn't know about. Do you think we should call Connor over here to help brainstorm?"

"Possibly later, but not just yet," said Aunt Alice. "Right now, you need to take Red Rover's ransom to the library. And while you're there, tell Tim and Debbie that they're to meet you here for the debriefing. I'm going to spend the afternoon on the Internet. By five, I hope I may have some useful information for you."

"I don't have the ransom," Bruce said miserably.

"But I do," Aunt Alice told him. "I was a big winner last night at bingo. I haven't had time to take the cash to the bank yet. It's in the top drawer of my bureau. Andi, I think you should be the one to go get it. It isn't appropriate for a boy to paw through a lady's undergarments."

So Andi got the money, and the two of them went to the library and tucked the bills between the pages of *Lassie Come Home*. Debbie was in the children's book room and Tim was in the main room, and they gave them Aunt Alice's message about meeting at her house. Then, with nothing else to do, they went to the park across the street and sat on a bench and watched as people went in and out of the library. It was hard to identify individuals at that distance. At one point Andi said, "I think that woman in the orange pants is Mrs. Tinkle," but there was no way to be certain.

It was a long afternoon. They all were exhausted when they finally reassembled in Aunt Alice's office.

"Is it five already?" Aunt Alice exclaimed. "I'd forgotten how quickly time passes when you're involved in a case. Is there news to report?"

"Nobody took money out of *The Incredible Journey*," Tim said. "I watched it all afternoon. But Mrs. Tinkle came in and went straight to the non-fiction section and took down a book called *All Things Bright and Beautiful*. After she left, I looked in that book and found two hundred dollars. We must have been right about the Tinkles getting a second ransom note. After that, I watched that book as well as the other one, but nobody came near either of them."

"I watched *Lassie Come Home* in the children's room," Debbie said. "Nobody came for that either. But Foxy's owner came in and left two hundred dollars in a book called *Good Dog, Carl.*"

"So we know that Foxy's been dognapped, too!" Andi exclaimed. "That makes five that we're sure of, including Red. The dognapper's getting rich!"

"Well, I have some interesting information," said Aunt Alice. "I've run a background check on Jerry's cousin, Connor."

"On *Connor!*" Bruce exclaimed. "But Connor's a good guy!"

"He does have a charming personality," Aunt Alice agreed. "However, he's also a con artist. Since Connor's a juvenile, I couldn't get access to his police record, but a lot of his classmates wrote about him on their personal Web sites. Back in Chicago, he and some friends were arrested for selling bogus magazine subscriptions. His older companions went to jail, but because of his age, Connor was sentenced to six months of community service. The judge agreed that he could do that in Elmwood, to get him away from the influence of evil companions. Connor wasn't brought to Elmwood to watch over Jerry. It's Jerry who's supposed to be supervising Connor."

"But Mr. Gordon told me —" Bruce paused as he tried to recall the statement. "Mr. Gordon said, 'Bad influences are a danger to vulnerable young people, and sometimes it takes a family effort to get them back on track.' I thought he was talking about Jerry, but he must have meant Connor! When I mentioned selling magazine subscriptions he got very upset. He said Connor used to do that but not anymore. He must not have known that Connor's selling them in Elmwood and Jerry's helping him."

"I looked up *Happy Housekeeping* on the Internet," Aunt Alice said. "I couldn't find it, and I'm wondering if it really exists."

"*Dogs' Home Journal* wasn't listed either," Bruce said. "Connor must have invented both those magazines!"

"But we don't have evidence to link them to the dognappings," Tim said. "Just because they're scam artists doesn't make them dognappers."

"There's nothing to link them directly," Aunt Alice agreed. "But there's an interesting coincidence in regard to Connor's volunteer work. He's doing his community service at the Elmwood library."

"At the library!" Andi gasped. "I've never seen him there, and I go there all the time!"

"He wouldn't be working up front," Aunt Alice said. "He'd be in the back room, rinsing out librarians' coffee cups."

"And shelving books and arranging chairs for story hour after the library closed for the night?" Andi asked.

"Very probably, yes. He's undoubtedly there after closing hour."

"Let's get him!" Tim cried. "We've got all we need to go to the police. Connor's prints must be in their database, and they can match them to the prints on Red's ransom note."

"No way!" Bruce said firmly. "What if Connor wore gloves? If Connor's prints aren't on the note, the cops will let him go, and we'll never see the dogs again. Connor and Jerry will leave them wherever they've put them, in a cellar or a garage —"

"Or a toolshed," Andi inserted. "In the book I'm writing, it's a toolshed."

"We'll get the dogs back, but first we'll have to find them," said Aunt Alice. "We need a spy to infiltrate the ranks of the enemy."

"I'm a spy!" Debbie cried. "I'll volunteer!"

"I'm afraid you're not quite right for the part," Aunt Alice told her. "This afternoon, while I was doing research, I found a Web site that described some intriguing gadgets. One is a recovery system for stolen vehicles. It sends out a silent signal that you can pick up on a computer through an online tracking service. It even tells you the speed a vehicle is traveling. I thought that sounded fascinating and ordered one. They're shipping it overnight, so I should have it in the morning."

"You're thinking of attaching a tracker to Connor's car?" Bruce asked.

"No," Aunt Alice said. "That thought did occur to me, but how do we know that Connor uses his car to visit the dogs? Maybe he has them hidden somewhere in the neighborhood and Jerry goes over on his skateboard to feed and water them."

"Or maybe they don't feed and water them at all," Andi said, cringing at the thought.

"There's only one way to find those dogs," Aunt Alice said. "There has to be another dognapping, but this time there will be a tracking device on the dog's collar."

"But how can we know what dog they'll take next?" Tim asked her.

"By criminal profiling," said Aunt Alice. "We need to figure out how the dognappers select their victims. Apparently most, if not all, of the dogs who were taken were featured in *The Bow-Wow News*. However, we know of at least two dogs who were prominently featured but weren't dognapped."

"Barkley and Snowflake," Andi said.

"So, the question is, why were those particular dogs passed over? What do they have in common that sets them apart?"

Everybody was silent for a moment, thinking.

Then Andi said, "Their owners may not love them enough to pay the ransom."

"That may be true of Barkley," Bruce said. "Mr. Murdock would probably be glad not to have to walk him. But Snowflake's a celebrity. The Swansons have her insured for fifty thousand dollars."

"Snowflake has competed in dog shows for eight years," Aunt Alice said. "One year in the life of a dog equals seven in the life of a human, so Snowflake is fifty-seven years old in people-time. She's well into middle age and no longer winning prizes. If the Swansons aren't emotionally attached to Snowflake, they probably wouldn't pay the ransom. They'd rather collect the insurance."

"Connor and Jerry are slick," Bruce said bitterly. "They only take dogs whose owners love them. So, to get them interested in staging another dognapping, we'll need to provide them with a victim whose owner is sure to pay the ransom. What kind of dog would that be?"

"Well," Aunt Alice said slowly, "the most precious dog I can imagine would belong to an elderly widow. A lady who lives alone and is in need of companionship. A dog like that might command quite a lot of ransom, especially if that particular lady was known throughout the neighborhood for raking in money at bingo."

"You're talking about *you*?" Andi exclaimed. "But you're allergic to dogs!"

"I'm allergic to their *hair*," Aunt Alice told her. "If I had an opportunity to own a sweet hairless dog, I might enjoy that. Such dogs do exist. They're called Chinese cresteds. They don't shed at all and are perfect for allergy sufferers."

"Are you thinking about getting one?" Bruce asked her.

"I'm afraid it would take too long to order one from China," Aunt Alice said. "If we want to close this case quickly — and we're all agreed that we do — then we'll have to manufacture a Chinese crested ourselves."

CHAPTER FOURTEEN

"Absolutely not!" Andi shrieked. "There's no way that I'm going to shave Friday!"

"You don't have a choice," Bruce told her. "She's our only candidate. Jerry would recognize MacTavish from back when he was a stray and used to hang out behind the school cafeteria. And he'd recognize Bebe, because Debbie's been walking her past his house to take her to the Doggie Park. The only dog that Jerry doesn't know about is Friday."

"She'll be so ashamed!" cried Andi. "She's so shy already, think how she'll feel if she doesn't have any hair! How would you feel if somebody cut your hair off?"

"I wouldn't like it," Bruce admitted. "But I'd put up with it if it would save lives. Red and Friday are like brother and sister. They share the same home.

Would Friday risk Red's life just so she could stay furry?"

"You won't need to shave her whole body," Aunt Alice said. "Chinese cresteds are hairless except for their heads, feet, and tails. You can leave tufts of hair on Friday's tail and around her ankles and a patch on top of her head. I printed a picture from the Internet, so you'll have that to go by. Personally, I'd prefer to have a totally bald dog, but I'll have to make do with what's available. I will take an allergy pill and put Friday on a very long leash when I walk her."

"Debbie?" Andi turned desperately to her friend for support. "You don't agree with them, do you? You don't want your best friend's dog to become a social misfit?"

"Sorry, Andi," Debbie said sympathetically, "but I really do think you have to do this. Besides, Friday's already a social misfit. This isn't going to make her any more of one."

"It's not that big a deal," Tim said. "She's not going to stay bald forever. Just think, when her hair grows back she's going to be a heroine. We can give her Trixie's medal that says 'World's Best Dog.'"

"I hate this," Andi muttered miserably. "I hate it, hate it, hate it."

Unable to face the prospect of performing the act herself, she sat on the closed lid of the toilet in the Walkers' bathroom with a towel spread over her lap and Friday on the towel. She closed her eyes and listened to the ominous buzz as Bruce ran an electric razor over Friday's back and down her legs. Mr. Walker's razor had gone to Europe with him, so Tim had borrowed his father's, which he hoped he'd be able to return before it was missed.

Andi would never have imagined how much hair Friday had until she saw it piled on the towel. And, having always thought of Friday as just as chubby as Bebe, she never would have guessed how wretched and pink and pitiful Friday's scrawny little body was underneath the fluffy covering of fur.

"She looks a little bit like a plucked chicken," Bruce commented, and was immediately sorry. "A *cute* plucked chicken," he amended. "And that crest on her head looks sort of like a peacock's."

"The poor little thing!" Andi sobbed. "I just can't stand this!"

Bebe, who had been watching in horror from the doorway, bolted from the room, obviously fearful that she would be next.

Andi snatched up a second bath towel and wrapped it around Friday, cuddling her close.

"At least it's summer and she won't catch cold," Bruce said.

"She's shivering anyway," Andi told him. "She's trembling from shock and embarrassment. When this is over, she's going to need a dog psychologist."

When they took Friday over to Aunt Alice's, they took the long way around, circling the block and entering the house through the kitchen to avoid passing the Gordons' house, in case Jerry or Connor might be out in the front yard. They had noticed Connor's car in the driveway on their way to their own house, so they knew he was somewhere about and that Jerry was probably with him.

"So, here is our dear little spy!" Aunt Alice said when Andi carried Friday in to her. "Let's unveil her and see what we have to work with."

Reluctantly, Andi removed the towel, revealing Friday in her entirety, while Aunt Alice regarded the dog in stunned fascination.

"My gracious!" she said. "Let's hope the sacrifice is worth it. She *does* resemble the Chinese crested on the Internet. I didn't realize Friday's 'crest' would be quite so pronounced, though. My eyes are starting to water and I haven't even touched her."

"What's that box over there on the table?" Bruce asked her.

"I was just getting ready to point that out to you," said Aunt Alice. "It's the box for the tracking device. I couldn't understand the instructions, so I asked Tim to take it up to my office and figure out how it works. Once he gets it linked to my computer, we should be able to track the location of the portable unit by watching the blips on the monitor."

"I'll go help him!" Bruce said eagerly.

"Not now, dear," Aunt Alice told him. "You have your own mission to complete before you and Tim can start experimenting with our new toy. You're going to have to take a picture of — this dog. We need to come up with a new name for her. What would you like to call her, Andi?"

"Lola," Andi said immediately. "If Friday looks awful in person, at least she can have a pretty name."

"Lola's a lovely name," Aunt Alice said approvingly. "Bruce, run home and get your camera so you can take a picture of Lola and me together. I suppose I'm going to have to be cuddling her in the picture so the dognappers will be able to see my devotion. I definitely will need an allergy pill for the photo session."

"Why do we need to take a picture?" Andi asked her, thinking how humiliating it would be for Friday to have her hairlessness a matter of record.

"For *The Bow-Wow News*, of course," Aunt Alice said. "How else will the dognappers know that Lola exists, much less how much I adore her?"

Bruce couldn't believe what he was hearing. "But you promised Mom and Dad that you wouldn't let us publish the paper!"

"I won't," Aunt Alice said. "I will publish it myself. I'll need you to take the photograph, but I — and I alone — will put out this special edition. My name will appear on the masthead as publisher and editor — in tiny letters, of course, so nobody can read it. Not that the Gordon boys will read that anyway. All their attention will be focused on the article and picture."

"How many copies are we going to print?" Debbie asked her.

"Not 'we,' dear — I," Aunt Alice told her. "I will print a single copy. That's all we're going to need — just one lone copy for Bruce to deliver to Connor. Now, let's get to work. Tim is deciphering the instructions for our tracking device. Debbie, I'm going to need you to supply material for the second page of this issue. It would seem suspicious if it was blank.

"Bruce, run home and get your camera while I take my allergy pill. There's a term detectives use when they get an instinctive feeling about a case. They call that feeling 'the Blue Sense.' Right now, I'm getting a Blue Sense feeling that we need to get moving very fast."

When Bruce reached the sidewalk and turned toward his own house, he saw Jerry and Connor approaching from that direction. Connor was striding along with his hands in his pockets, and Jerry was cruising beside him on his skateboard.

"Hi, Bruce!" Connor called with a friendly smile. "I saw a UPS truck in your aunt's driveway. What's that nice old lady up to these days? Is she ordering stuff from eBay?"

"Actually," Bruce said, "she just bought herself a dog."

"A dog!" Jerry exclaimed. "Do you really expect us to believe that? I've lived next door to Mrs. Scudder all my life. She's so allergic to dogs that she won't go near one."

"This is a special, very valuable dog," Bruce told him, longing to leap at Jerry and knock him off his skateboard. "It's a Chinese crested, especially bred for people with allergies. Lola — that's what her name is — was delivered this morning. Aunt Alice is crazy about her. She's sent me home to get my camera so I can take a picture for *The Bow-Wow News*."

"I heard a rumor that you were going out of business," Connor said.

"Nope," Bruce said. "We fell slightly behind in production, but the new issue will be out tomorrow. Speaking of which, Aunt Alice says she hasn't been receiving that homemaking magazine she ordered from you. Do you know when it's going to start coming?"

"No way to tell," Jerry said. "Connor and I just sell subscriptions; we're not responsible for delivery. Maybe the publisher 'fell slightly behind in production,' or the magazine's been lost in the mail. How is my old buddy, Red Rover? I haven't seen him around lately."

"I promised my dad I won't run him until he and Mom get back from their trip," Bruce said. "Well, guys, I've got to be going. I have to get my camera and take Lola's picture."

Even though he knew that it wasn't going to happen, when he entered his yard Bruce experienced one heady instant of wild expectation that a big red dog might come flying to greet him. After all, he had left the ransom exactly as requested, and Connor and Jerry had been coming from the direction of his house. There was a chance — though a slim one — that they might have returned Red Rover to his own backyard.

But he knew in his heart that they hadn't, because how could they? The only way to transport a dog the size of Red was by car, and Connor and Jerry had been on foot. Still, his own Blue Sense told him that the boys had been coming from his house and that, moments ago, they had been here in the very yard where he was now standing.

Although his heart sank at the sight, he was not surprised to see a sheet of paper taped to the roof of

Red's doghouse. This time he didn't immediately remove it. Instead, he went into the house to get his camera.

Bebe was huddled in the corner of the living room sofa, looking lonely and dejected.

"Hi, Bebe," Bruce said, feeling sorry for her. "Come over here and see Uncle Bruce. Andi is going to be coming over later to play with you."

However, instead of running to him, Bebe leapt off the sofa and went scurrying into the laundry room, where she wedged herself behind the dryer. She apparently feared he'd come back to administer another haircut.

Bruce didn't attempt to pursue her. Instead, he went upstairs to get his camera. From his bedroom window he could look out across the backyard and over the gate to the street. If only he had been here ten minutes earlier, he would have had a clear shot of Connor and Jerry as they entered the yard and taped the note to the doghouse!

Well, too late now, he told himself, going back downstairs and out through the kitchen door, locking it carefully behind him. Then he crossed the yard to the doghouse and took a series of pictures. Finally, when he was satisfied that he had sufficient evidence to support his claim that the note was taped to the doghouse, he peeled it from the roof, once again being careful to touch only the edges.

His blood ran cold as he read the message:

THE FIRST INSTALLMENT OF THE RANSOM HAS BEEN RECEIVED. THE SECOND INSTALLMENT IS NOW DUE. LEAVE AN ADDITIONAL $276 IN A COPY OF <u>WHITE FANG</u> AT THE ELMWOOD LIBRARY. ONCE AGAIN, BE WARNED NOT TO GO TO THE POLICE. IF YOU DO, YOU WON'T GET YOUR DOG BACK. ONLY HIS EARS.

His *ears*!

The vision of Red's beautiful floppy ears, flying behind him like long red streamers when they went on runs, was enough to fill Bruce with both terror and fury. Where was he going to get another $276? He couldn't keep borrowing from Aunt Alice, even if she had the money, and he wasn't sure that she did. After all, she had just bought the tracking device.

It was all Bruce could do to prevent himself from going straight to the Bernsteins' house to borrow their son's baseball bat and go from there to the

Gordons' house and knock both boys senseless. But the aftermath of a scene like that would be disastrous. Connor and Jerry would end up in the hospital and would then appear on the witness stand, testifying pathetically through their bandages that they were victims of "an unprovoked attack by a madman." Bruce would spend years in a juvenile detention center, while his parents wasted away from shame and sorrow. And, worst of all, the captive dogs would be left to starve in some deserted garage or basement with nobody knowing they were there.

No, Aunt Alice's plan was the only way to go. And, wild as it was, the plan might actually work. But only if none of them slipped up, the tracking device was efficient, and Connor and Jerry were gullible and greedy enough to believe a far-fetched newspaper story that nobody saw except them.

"Hang in there, Red!" Bruce whispered. "Help is on the way!"

He slung his camera strap around his neck and, clutching the ransom note by one corner, set off down the street to Aunt Alice's house to do his part to put the plan into action.

CHAPTER FIFTEEN

CHINESE DOG TO BECOME CITIZEN OF ELMWOOD

Lola, a Chinese crested, has moved to Elmwood.

Mrs. Alice Scudder, Lola's new owner, says Lola is extraordinary.

"I've always longed for a dog," Mrs. Scudder said, "but I haven't been able to have one because of my allergies. I'm not allergic to Lola, because she doesn't have hair. Lola is a wonderful companion. Now that I have Lola, I can't imagine life without her."

Mrs. Scudder said it was expensive to import Lola from China, but she was able to afford it.

"I am very lucky at bingo," Mrs. Scudder said modestly.

People at the Senior Citizens Center who were interviewed for this article said Mrs. Scudder yells "Bingo!" more often than anybody else.

"Every time Alice comes to bingo she goes home rich," one of them said. "I'm sure she will spend her life savings to keep Lola safe and happy here in the United States."

Bruce's photo showed Aunt Alice sitting in a chair in her living room with Friday on her lap. Friday looked peculiar but surprisingly exotic. The tufts on her ankles puffed out in an interesting manner and her tail had a lovely tassel. But most impressive of all was the crest on her head. As Bruce had commented, it did look a bit like a peacock, and Friday was holding her head high as if posing for the camera.

She looks proud! Andi thought in astonishment when she saw the picture. Was it possible that Friday actually *liked* being bald?

At the time of the photo shoot, Aunt Alice's allergy pill hadn't fully kicked in yet, and her eyes were teary and her nose was running. However, the problems were easy to take care of. Bruce was able to digitally remove the nasal drip, and Andi's caption read, *"Alice Scudder sheds tears of joy because she is no longer lonely."*

The second page of the paper was more of a problem. Debbie couldn't construct a gossip column when the dogs who were her usual subjects were missing. So they printed some dog-friendly recipes, including Aunt Alice's recipe for quiche, which, if dog biscuits were substituted for broccoli, was surprisingly healthy. And Andi contributed the first chapter of her novel, which she had titled *Bobby Strikes Back.*

"This should do the trick," Aunt Alice said approvingly as she reviewed the lone copy of the paper. "Bruce, please take this over to Connor. And while you're at it, take Lola along on her leash. That way he and Jerry will see how remarkable she is."

Connor's car was not in the driveway when Bruce made his delivery, and Mr. Gordon was the one who came to the door.

"I'll give this to Connor," he said when Bruce handed him the paper. "He's out again tonight, doing volunteer work, and I'm delighted to say Jerry's with him. Jerry's mother and I would be very happy if our son decided to invest himself in good works. Connor made a few false starts, as many young people do, but there has been an amazing transformation in him this summer. I like to think it's the wholesome atmosphere in Elmwood. It's been a great experience for Jerry to watch that happen."

Then Mr. Gordon happened to glance down and see Lola.

"Good Lord, Bruce, what is *that*?" he asked in astonishment. "I've never seen anything like it! Why are you walking that animal and not Red Rover?"

"Dad told me not to take Red out while he and Mom are gone," Bruce said. "This is Aunt Alice's dog, Lola. You can read all about her in *The Bow-Wow News*. I'm giving her a little exercise before she goes to bed."

When he returned to Aunt Alice's, he found her with Andi in the living room, making a list of things that needed to be done before the dognapping.

"What should I do about the second ransom note?" Bruce asked her. "Connor and Jerry are at the library this very minute, probably looking in

White Fang. What will they do when they find out I didn't leave the money?"

"They won't find that out because the book isn't there," Aunt Alice told him. "I asked Debbie to stop by the library and check it out. Connor has no way of knowing if you paid the ransom. And by tomorrow he'll have read *The Bow-Wow News* and will be so excited about the prospect of dognapping Lola that Red Rover will be at the bottom of his to-do list. The challenge that faces us now is setting up the heist. We need to figure out the dognappers' schedule. What time of day do they usually snatch their victims?"

"Connor works at the library in the mornings and evenings," Bruce said. "We don't know about Ginger, because the Tinkles won't talk to us, but Bully and Trixie and Red all were snatched in the afternoon."

"Then that's when we'll need to make Lola available," Aunt Alice said. "I'm glad of that, since I don't enjoy getting up early."

"Where are you going to take her to be kidnapped?" Andi asked.

"There's no place like home," Aunt Alice said. "I was thinking I might take her out in the yard with me while I weed my flower beds."

"She'll get sunburned!" Andi objected. "Her skin's like a newborn baby's!"

"We'll cover her with sunblock," said Aunt Alice. "I might even set up an umbrella so she can sit in the shade. I'll work in the garden for a short while, and then my phone will ring. I'll leave the front door standing open and turn up the ringer volume, so the dognappers will be sure to hear it. I'll rush inside to answer it, just as Mr. Bernstein did when Bully was taken, and Lola will be left unguarded for a few vital minutes. That should give the Gordon boys time to snatch her."

"How do you know the phone will ring?" Andi asked her.

"Because you will call my home phone from my cell phone," Aunt Alice said. "We'll take that cell phone with us when we follow the dognappers. Tim will track them on the computer and tell Debbie the route they're taking, and Debbie will give you that information by phone. You and Bruce will come in the car with me, and Bruce will bring his camera to document the dogs' imprisonment. This will require a team effort."

"Are you sure the tracking device will work?" Bruce asked anxiously.

"It appears to be operating perfectly," Aunt Alice assured him. "There's a tiny gadget that Tim will attach to Lola's collar, which will send out a silent signal. That signal shows up as blinking dots on my computer screen. Tim will be able to tell us Lola's exact location, and we can follow her to her destination. Hopefully, we'll find the other dogs there as well."

That night, Andi slept with Friday-Lola snuggled next to her for the first time in over two weeks. It was a strange feeling, after having been used to sleeping with two cuddly dogs, to find herself sleeping with a hairless one. She had trouble falling asleep because she was worried about Bebe, all alone in the house at the end of the block. How vast and lonely that house must seem to one small dog all by herself!

Late that afternoon, she had taken Lola to visit Bebe, thinking that would be a treat for both of them, but to her dismay they had treated each other like strangers. Lola had marched in like a princess visiting the home of a peasant, and Bebe had refused to come out of the laundry room. Andi had knelt on the floor and extracted the unhappy dachshund from behind the dryer and brushed off the lint and tried to comfort her.

"You can't go with us to Aunt Alice's tonight," Andi told her. "Not unless we shave you, and you don't want that. You'll just have to tough it out here a little while longer."

But despite having had it explained to her, Bebe raced to the door when Andi started to leave with Lola, as if she expected to go with them. When she realized they were leaving without her, she looked so sad and disappointed that Andi, recalling the look on the little dog's face, felt as if her heart would break.

Bruce also was having a hard time sleeping. He kept picturing Red Rover and his beautiful ears. Aunt Alice's idea of having Debbie check *White Fang* out of the library had been an inspiration, but what if there was more than one copy? Or what if Connor decided to use the library's computer to pull up information about who checked the book out? He might not know Debbie was Andi's best friend, but Jerry did.

Although earlier he had been excited about the thought of tomorrow's heist, suddenly Bruce was filled with misgivings. So many things could go wrong! What if the tracking system didn't work? Or Connor or Jerry noticed the device on Lola's collar? Or Aunt Alice's computer crashed? And above all, what if Connor and Jerry caught on to the plan? Connor was a practiced scam artist. How could he believe the article in the paper when it was so obviously a fake? Wouldn't somebody with Connor's unscrupulous background recognize such an amateurish setup when he saw one?

When Aunt Alice came downstairs the next morning, Bruce and Andi were waiting at the kitchen table.

"I'm scared," Bruce said without apology. "This scheme we've cooked up is too transparent. Connor and Jerry can't possibly be taken in by it."

"Don't upset yourself, dear," Aunt Alice said, switching on the coffeemaker. "We have a secret weapon that makes us invincible. Do either of you want an egg?"

"Not me," Bruce said. "I'm too worried to eat a thing."

"I'd like an egg," Andi said. "Why won't they suspect us? What's our secret weapon?"

"My age," Aunt Alice said.

Andi regarded her with bewilderment. "I don't understand."

"I'm old," Aunt Alice said placidly. "Old people aren't taken seriously. Connor is far too cocky and egotistical to think that a white-haired lady would try to put one over on him. Bruce, I'm going to fix you an egg regardless. You're going to need your energy."

So Bruce forced down a breakfast he had no desire for, and Andi ate two fried eggs and a sweet roll and went down the street to visit Bebe. Aunt Alice finished her coffee and went off to put gas in her car.

"Who knows where those boys may be keeping the dogs?" she said. "We may have to follow them all the way into the next county."

Connor's Miata was gone from the Gordons' driveway all morning but returned around noon, and Andi, who had been keeping watch from Aunt Alice's office window, saw both Jerry and Connor get out of the car and go into the house. She wondered if it was significant that Jerry had taken to accompanying Connor to the library. *He's probably eager to get his share of the money*, she speculated.

Shortly before 3 P.M., when Lola had been slathered with sunblock and Aunt Alice was putting on her gardening gloves, Tim suddenly cried, "We're missing something important! We're going to need a second cell phone!"

"We'll take mine in the car with us," Aunt Alice said. "Debbie can use my home phone to pass along your directions." Then she gasped and said, "How scatterbrained can I be! My computer connects to the Internet through my phone line! You won't be able to use that phone when the computer's on!"

"I didn't think of that either," Bruce said. "We've got to get another cell phone." He turned to Tim and Debbie. "Do either of you have one at your house?"

"Dad has one, but he takes it to work," Tim said.

Debbie said, "Mom would never let me have hers. She talks on it every ten minutes — even at the grocery store."

"Mrs. Bernstein has a cell phone," Aunt Alice said. "I saw her use it when she called her husband from Garden Club."

"I'll run over there now and see if I can borrow it," Andi said. "I'll be right back. It should only take me a minute."

But when she got to the Bernsteins', she found the couple so distraught that she was unable to break away before hearing the whole awful story of Bully's third ransom note.

"I met their demands and delivered the second payment," Mr. Bernstein said. "I put it in *The Incredible Journey* like they told me. But they still didn't bring Bully back. Then, yesterday, we found a third note stuck through our mail slot. They wanted another two hundred!"

"Did you pay it?" Andi asked.

"Of course," Mrs. Bernstein said. "What choice did we have?"

"The problem is that now we can't pay our bills," Mr. Bernstein said. "We're sitting here waiting for our utilities to be shut off. I guess we can live without electricity, but what if they want a fourth payment? What will we do then?"

"We're going to get the dogs back today," Andi told them. "At least, we're going to try. But in order to do that, I'll need to borrow your cell phone. I can't go into the reason, it's just too complicated. But could I please borrow it, just for this afternoon?"

"I'll get it for you right now," Mrs. Bernstein said. "Is there anything else we can lend you — anything at all?"

Andi thought for a moment about asking to borrow the baseball bat, but then decided against it. The Bernsteins' son had probably been as gentle a person as his parents. It didn't seem right to use something he had owned as a weapon.

CHaPTeR SiXTeeN

When Andi returned to Aunt Alice's house, which they now all referred to as "Headquarters," she took the roundabout route that she and Bruce had determined was the only way to come and go undetected by the Gordon boys. She entered through the kitchen and immediately went upstairs. Bruce, Tim, and Debbie were gathered in Aunt Alice's office, glued to what was going on beneath the window.

When Andi joined them, she said, "Let me see, too!"

"So, you're finally back!" Bruce said. "What took you so long? Aunt Alice and Lola are probably burned to a crisp, sunblock or not."

"I couldn't get back sooner," Andi said. "The Bernsteins had to pay a third ransom, and now they don't have enough money to pay their bills. So of course, I had to listen to them and comfort them. I promised them we'd get Bully back for them today. *Now* can I look out the window?"

"There's not much to see," Debbie said, stepping back to make room for her. "Your aunt Alice is digging up weeds, and Lola is sitting under the umbrella, sweating."

"Dogs don't sweat," Andi said. "The drip comes out through their tongues."

"Well, she looks like she's sweating," Debbie said, and, when Andi looked out the window, she had to agree. Lola's little body was glistening. Andi hoped it was the sunscreen.

"Here's the Bernsteins' cell phone," she told Debbie, handing it over. "I'll use Aunt Alice's now to call her home number. But —" Suddenly she realized there was a glaring hole in the scene that she was gazing down at. "Connor's car isn't in the Gordons' driveway!"

"He parked it at the end of the street," Bruce said. "See it there at the corner? He moved it ten minutes ago."

"Why would he do that?" Andi asked as she spotted the car, parked about three houses down.

"Mrs. Gordon can see the driveway from their kitchen window," Tim said. "Connor and Jerry can't risk her watching them take off. What if she started calling, 'Where are you going? Please stop at the store and pick up a loaf of bread'? What if Aunt Alice came back from taking her phone call and saw their car tear out of the driveway next door? They've got to have that car positioned somewhere else."

"Then they're really going to do this!" Andi said. "It's not just something we've dreamed up, like a chapter in my novel. This is *real*!"

"This is real," Bruce agreed. "Are you ready to start things rolling?"

"I'm dialing right now," Andi told him.

A few seconds later, Aunt Alice's home phone began ringing. The ringer was turned up so high that Andi jumped when she heard it. From the window they could see Aunt Alice rising slowly and rather stiffly from her kneeling position at the edge of the flower bed.

She cupped her ear and asked Lola, "Was that the phone?"

The phone rang again, and Andi felt sure that neighbors blocks away must have heard it.

"I believe that's my phone," Aunt Alice told Lola loudly. "I'm expecting a call from my nephew and his wife in Europe. I'm going to have to leave you out here alone, dear, so be sure to stay under the umbrella. Auntie Alice loves you and doesn't want you to get sunburned. Auntie Alice will be right back, as soon as she can get those bothersome relatives off the line."

Aunt Alice turned and went into the house. She picked up the living room phone and commanded, "Everyone to your post! Tim at the computer! Debbie next to him with the Bernsteins' cell phone! Andi and Bruce to the car with my cell phone and Bruce's camera!"

"Get away from the window," Bruce told them. "I'm going to try to get a picture of the dognapping."

He barely had time to step into place before it happened. One moment Lola was lolling on a beach towel in the shade of a striped umbrella, and an instant later she was gone.

"I got it!" Bruce cried. "I caught the dognappers in the act!" But when he brought the image up on the screen on the back of his camera, he moaned with disappointment. "All you can see are two guys in black T-shirts and baseball caps. Their heads are turned so their faces don't show."

"Don't worry about it," Tim said. "You'll get pictures of them later. Look — we can already start tracking Lola on the monitor! *Blip — blip — blip* — now the dot has stopped and is holding steady — they must be putting her into Connor's car. Now the dot's moving again — he must be pulling away."

"He is!" Debbie cried, pushing in beside Bruce to get a better look. "He's whipping around the corner and heading north!" An instant later she said, "I've lost sight of them."

"But I haven't! I can see them fine!" Tim was bursting with excitement. "There they go — they're on Locust Street, zipping along. You guys better get a move on. This is so cool! It's like a computer game, except the bad guys are real!"

When Andi and Bruce reached the driveway, Aunt Alice was already revving up the engine of her car.

"Hurry and get in," she cried. "Andi, I'll need you in the passenger's seat since you'll be the navigator. Could Tim tell which direction they were headed?"

"They turned north on Locust," Bruce said, leaping into the backseat. "But maybe they're trying to throw us off."

"I doubt that," said Aunt Alice. "There's no way they can know they're being followed. They just want to leave the scene of the crime as fast as possible."

The cell phone rang and Andi quickly punched the TALK button.

"They're headed for the freeway," Debbie told her. "They haven't reached the ramp yet, so Tim doesn't know if they're going to head east or west. He says hold back for a minute until he can tell you. You don't want to get yourself trapped going the wrong direction." She was silent a moment and then said, "They're approaching the ramp. Now they're on the freeway. Tim says they're headed east at sixty-five miles an hour."

"East on the freeway," Andi cried, and Aunt Alice pulled onto the eastbound ramp.

"Can't you go any faster?" Bruce asked frantically.

"There's no reason to," Aunt Alice said. "We're not trying to keep them in sight, and there's no way I want to risk getting stopped by a state trooper."

They continued on down the freeway for fifteen minutes. Then Debbie told Andi, "Tim says they're turning left onto an exit ramp that leads to River Road."

"That's about a mile ahead of us," Aunt Alice said when Andi conveyed that information. "If we turn west on that road, we'll end up at the Black Rock River, but I don't know what we'll find in the other direction."

"Oh, not a *river*!" Andi gasped, her mind filled with visions of helpless dogs being dropped off a bridge into churning rapids.

"Do you think they're drowning the dogs?!" Bruce asked in horror, his own mind following the same thought process. They could be doing exactly that. Since they weren't returning the dogs, why wouldn't they drown them so they wouldn't have to feed and take care of them?

"They would never do that," Aunt Alice said reassuringly. "There would be too much publicity when the bodies washed up on the shore."

"Not if they weighed them down with sand-bags," Andi said.

"Connor's car is too small to carry sandbags," Aunt Alice said. "Believe me, children, those dogs are *not* in the river."

Debbie's voice spoke so suddenly into Andi's ear that she almost jumped out of her seat. "They've turned east on River Road!"

"They're going *east*!" Andi shouted ecstatically, and Bruce sighed with relief. No matter what lay to the east, it wouldn't be the river.

A sign saying RIVER ROAD EXIT appeared up ahead of them.

Aunt Alice pulled into the exit lane, and a moment later they were down the ramp and on a two-lane road that ran parallel to the freeway.

"They've turned north onto Valley Road," Debbie said. "They've slowed down to forty miles an hour. It's like they're getting ready to —"

Her voice broke off, and there was silence.

"Oh, no!" Andi exclaimed. "The battery's gone dead!"

"It can't have," Aunt Alice said. "I recharged it last night."

"Then the problem must be with the Bernsteins' phone," Andi said. "They've been so worried about Bully that the last thing on their minds was recharging their cell phone."

"Well, the phone got us this far anyway," Aunt Alice said. "I'm glad I got gas, because we *are* in the next county. Judging by where we were when Tim said they left the freeway, we're approximately a mile behind them."

She had followed Tim's last instructions and turned north onto a winding country road that was flanked with the lushness of summer. If it hadn't been for the seriousness of their situation, the drive would have been delightful. Fields of alfalfa and clover, sprinkled with tiny purple blossoms, were interspersed with wheat fields. Picturesque barns and silos dotted the horizon, and the slanted afternoon sunlight cast a golden haze over everything. An occasional dirt lane or unpaved driveway ran between the fields, curving back behind them in the direction of a barn or farmhouse.

"You'd better floor it," Bruce told Aunt Alice. "The only way we can find them now is to catch up with them. Debbie said they reduced their speed."

"That's what concerns me," Aunt Alice said. "Why would they suddenly do that? Tell me again, Andi — what exactly did Debbie say to you?"

"She said, 'They've slowed down to forty miles an hour,'" Andi said, trying to recall Debbie's precise wording. "Then she said, 'It's like they're getting ready to,' and that's when we were cut off."

"They're 'getting ready to' do what?" Bruce said. "There's nothing out here to get ready for. Nothing except —" He paused and then said slowly, "Nothing except to turn off onto one of those side lanes. But those don't appear to go anywhere except into farmland."

"Where there are barns and silos and toolsheds," Andi said. "Places that they could stash dogs."

"You're right," Aunt Alice said, bringing the car to a stop at the side of the road. "It's possible I may have come too far. Where were we when Debbie's call ended?"

"On River Road," Bruce said. "Then we turned onto Valley Road, which is what we're on now. If Connor was a mile ahead of us and was preparing to turn into a driveway, we did come too far. Now we'll never find them!"

"We'll find them," Aunt Alice promised, starting up her car again and making a U-turn. "We'll backtrack to River Road and start all over again."

They retraced the route they had just covered until the frontage road loomed ahead and they could hear the sound of cars on the freeway. Then, Aunt Alice made another U-turn, glanced at her mileage gauge, and began to drive slowly back down Valley Road.

"It's going to be about a mile to the spot where Connor slowed down," she said. "Keep an eye out for lanes and driveways they might have turned onto. There can't be many out here in the middle of nowhere."

But a mile down the road they discovered that there were more options than they had anticipated. Several lanes intersected on either side of the road, each of them shielded by wheat fields, so there was no way to tell where they went. Some might lead to farmhouses, others to outbuildings, and others might end at locked gates.

"What do we do now?" Andi asked miserably. The situation was unbearable. They knew the dogs were out here someplace, but where? Whichever lane they turned down stood a good chance of being the wrong one.

"Now is the time we must use the Blue Sense," Aunt Alice said. "Bruce, get out of the car and walk a short way down each of those lanes and see how you feel. You have a strong bond with Red Rover. Shut your eyes and call out to him with your mind.

Tell him you're trying to find him and ask him where he is."

"That's crazy," Bruce said, but even as he said it he was reaching for the door handle. Because this was their only option. If this didn't work, Red might be lost to him forever.

"Take as much time as you need," Aunt Alice told him. "If you don't feel anything on one lane, then walk down another. Whatever is going to happen is going to happen."

Bruce got out of the car and walked along the edge of the road to the spot where the lanes intersected. He stepped into the entrance of the nearest lane and closed his eyes. He stood there for a long time, mentally calling out to his dog, but he felt nothing. *This isn't going to work*, he told himself, but he kept on standing there, feeling foolish and ineffectual, calling silently, *Red! Red! Red!* Finally he became so frustrated, he went back to the car.

"You can't give up yet," Aunt Alice told him.

"Let Andi give it a try," Bruce said. "She has a relationship with Lola. Maybe the Blue Sense will work for her."

"You're more bonded to Red than I am to Lola," Andi said. "I was close to her when she was Friday, but her personality's changed. I don't know her at all as Lola. Please, Bruce, try that lane over there. You're our only hope now."

So Bruce crossed the road and entered a winding lane that led back into wheat fields. Again he closed his eyes and reached out to Red Rover with his mind, and again he felt nothing. But he stood there anyway, feeling the tension flow out of him as he allowed the peace and tranquility of his surroundings to encompass him. The sun was warm on his arms and on the back of his neck. The mesmerizing scents of summer were all around him, and suddenly the world that had seemed so silent was alive with sound. He was aware of the buzzing of bees and chanting of crickets. Birds were chirping and trilling, and somewhere in the distance he could hear the sound of a tractor.

He heard the lowing of a cow who wanted to be milked.

He heard the wail of a baby in some nearby farmhouse.

And then he heard a dog.

He heard the bark of a dog, and he knew that voice — it was as familiar to him as the voices of his parents and sister. *It was the voice of Red Rover!*

Bruce opened his eyes and the other sounds went away, because all he could concentrate on now was the voice of his dog. There were other dog voices in the background, but they were overshadowed by the voice he loved so well. That voice was coming from the left branch of the lane, and it was loud enough so he knew it was not far off.

He raced back to the car and tumbled into the backseat.

"I heard him!" he cried. "I heard Red! It's that lane over there! It forks when you get a few yards into it. We need to take the left fork to get to the dogs. I could hear them all barking."

"Is this the Blue Sense?" Andi asked, entranced by the fact that her skeptical brother had apparently suddenly become psychic. "Aunt Alice, does Bruce have the Blue Sense? How did he do this?"

"Bruce doesn't necessarily have the Blue Sense," Aunt Alice said. "We can't rule that out entirely, but it's much more likely that he simply walked down that lane and really started listening and heard the very real noise the dogs were making."

"So how does the Blue Sense fit into this?" Andi asked.

"It was the Blue Sense that caused me to send Bruce out there," Aunt Alice told her.

CHAPTER SEVENTEEN

Aunt Alice pulled into the lane that Bruce had indicated and took the fork to the left. Almost immediately they all could hear the dogs, and the barking grew increasingly louder as they bumped along the rutted road. Red Rover's rich voice was louder than any of the others. It was almost as if he could sense his master was coming.

At the end of the lane, a clearing appeared before them, and they found themselves looking at the remains of what once had been part of a small farm. There was a dilapidated barn with a roof that was missing whole sections and a door that was half off its hinges. A rusted tractor served as a trellis for a tangle of vines, and a rotted wagon slumped dejectedly next to a drainage ditch. It was clear that the place had been deserted for a very long time.

In startling contrast, a shiny silver Miata was

pulled up so close to the barn that its bumper almost touched it. Aunt Alice made a sharp turn and brought her own car to a stop, parking it broadside directly behind Connor's car.

"You're going to have to climb out on the driver's side," she told Andi. "There won't be room for you to get out the passenger's door."

Bruce had already leapt from the car and was racing around the side of the barn. As the dogs caught sight of him, the din of their voices became deafening.

"They're here!" Bruce shouted. "Bully and Trixie and Lola and a whole bunch of others! *And Red!*"

As Andi and Aunt Alice rounded the corner of the barn, they saw that the dogs were confined in a wire enclosure in front of a chicken house. At Bruce's approach, they had gone wild with excitement and were hurling themselves against the mesh. Bully and Ginger leapt up and down in unison, obviously having renewed their friendship. The only dog who wasn't jumping was Lola. She was standing apart from the others, pink and smug-looking. She seemed proud of the part she had played in the rescue mission, and she clearly expected to receive the "World's Best Dog" medal.

"There's a padlock on the gate!" Bruce cried. "We've got to get it off!"

"First you have to take pictures," Aunt Alice told him. "We need a photographic record of all the evidence."

"Well, what do you know!"

It was a voice that Bruce knew all too well, and it came from directly behind him. He turned and saw Jerry Gordon, holding a sack of dry dog food. Jerry was dressed in the same black T-shirt and baseball cap as the faceless person that Bruce had photographed snatching Lola, but now the cap was pushed back and his face was visible. Keeping his eyes locked on Jerry's so as not to indicate what he was doing, Bruce slid his hand down to rest on his camera and surreptitiously started clicking the shutter.

"Connor, you'll never believe this, but we've got company!" Jerry called out.

"Well, this is a surprise!" exclaimed Connor, materializing behind Jerry in the doorway of the barn. He, too, wore a black T-shirt and baseball cap, and his smile was as sunny as always. "It's Bruce and his sister and Mrs. Scudder! You must have received the same information we did!"

"What information?" Andi asked him.

"We had a call from an anonymous tipster," Connor told her. "He said a bunch of stray dogs were trapped in a chicken yard and no one was taking care of them. We drove out here to bring the dogs food."

"And how did you think you were going to get to them?" Bruce asked him. "I guess you must have a key to unlock the gate?"

"A key?" Connor responded innocently. "How could we have that? We don't know where those dogs came from or how they got in there. We were thinking about tossing dog food in through the mesh, but that might make me late for my volunteer work. Now that you're here, you can feed them. Maybe later we can figure out a way to get that lock off."

"I want the key!" Bruce insisted, trailing the two around to the front of the barn. "You locked those dogs in there, and you can get them out!"

"You heard Connor," Jerry told him. "We don't have a key, and we don't have any idea how those dogs got trapped there. We'll leave the dog food with you, but we've got to get going. Connor has business to tend to."

"I bet he does," Andi murmured bitterly to Aunt Alice. "And I bet it has to do with taking money out of library books."

"Don't worry, dear," Aunt Alice said softly, so only Andi could hear her. "Those two are not going anywhere until we allow it."

A moment later Connor shouted, "Mrs. Scudder, come move your car! You've got me blocked and I can't back out!"

"I'm terribly sorry," Aunt Alice said as she and Andi joined the boys at the front of the barn. "I never was very good at parking."

"Give me the keys, and I'll move it myself," Connor told her.

"I don't have the keys," said Aunt Alice.

"You must have the keys," Connor said impatiently. "You drove in here, didn't you?"

"Perhaps I dropped them when I got out of the car," Aunt Alice said. "With all the commotion those noisy animals were making, I got a bit rattled. Why don't you and Jerry search the ground on the driver's side? Andi, see if I left them in the ignition."

"What about your purse?" Connor demanded, his voice rising in exasperation. "Women always put their keys in their purses."

"I don't know where my purse is either," Aunt Alice said. "It's a slippery purse and it sometimes slides out of my hands. Andi, while you're in there looking for the car keys, please see if I dropped my purse."

"Why don't you just ram her car and shove it over?" Jerry suggested to Connor.

"Why, Jerry!" Aunt Alice gasped. "I can't believe what I'm hearing! You're encouraging your cousin to ram your neighbor's car? I'm afraid that Connor has not been a very good influence."

"I'm not about to dent my Miata!" Connor cried, getting more and more furious by the minute. "Do you know how much that baby cost me?"

"You must have sold a lot of subscriptions to be able to afford such a lovely vehicle," Aunt Alice said. "On that subject, I still haven't started receiving *Happy Housekeeping.* I've been looking forward so much to reading that magazine, because I'm thinking of redecorating my living room. Jerry, you've been in my home. Do you think it needs redecorating?"

"Enough of this babble!" Connor shouted. "I want those keys!"

He stormed over to Aunt Alice's car, yanked the driver's door open, and dragged Andi out. She kicked futilely at his legs and tried to jab him with her elbow.

"Let go of me!" she cried. "You're hurting my arm!"

"Give me the keys!" Connor said.

"They weren't in the ignition," Andi told him. "But I did find Aunt Alice's purse. It was under the seat. Here, Aunt Alice — *catch*!"

Jerking free of his grip, she tossed the purse to her great-aunt, who made an amazingly good catch as Connor again grabbed Andi's arm.

"Let go of her, Connor," Aunt Alice said. "I will search in my purse for the keys. But before I do that, I must take an allergy pill. So many dogs held together like this is overwhelming to someone allergic to dog hair."

"That's another ploy and I'm not going to fall for it!" Connor yelled, losing his cool altogether. "You're not the sweet ditzy old lady that everyone thinks you are! For all I know, you have a gun in that purse!"

He made a lunge for Aunt Alice and, grabbing her purse with one hand, shoved her hard with the other. Aunt Alice's feet shot out from under her and she tumbled heavily backward onto the ground.

"What have you done, you idiot?" Andi screamed at Connor, dropping to her knees beside her great-aunt. "Now you're not just guilty of dognapping but assault and purse snatching, too! They're going to drag you back to Chicago in handcuffs!"

"That's not going to happen," Connor said, back in control again now that he had what he wanted. "Mrs. Scudder slipped and fell. Old people do that. I've got Jerry as a witness, and people always believe Jerry. He's got the Gordon charm and can use it just like I can."

He dug through Aunt Alice's purse until he found her car keys. Tossing the purse on the ground, he got into her car and deliberately backed it into the side of the tractor.

Then he jumped out of her car and into his own.

"Come on, Jerry!" he yelled. "You and I are out of here!"

Jerry glanced at Aunt Alice, who was lying flat on her back staring up at the sky. Her chest was rising and falling in a frightening manner, and she seemed to be gasping for air.

He said, "Mrs. Scudder, this wasn't supposed to happen. No one was meant to get hurt, not even the dogs. Connor got carried away. I'm sorry about that."

"It's a little too late to be sorry," Bruce said angrily. "You'll never be able to make up for all the pain you've caused people." He picked up Aunt Alice's purse and rummaged through it until he found her vial of allergy medicine.

"I'm not guilty of anything," Jerry said. "I'm not the one who roughed up your sister and aunt."

"You've hurt more people than you can possibly know," Bruce told him. "You don't have to injure them physically to tear their hearts out."

"It was just a prank," Jerry said. "You have no sense of humor. When I get home, I'll call a taxi to come and get you. I hope Mrs. Scudder's all right, but I'll stand by Connor — she lost her balance and fell. Connor wasn't anywhere near her."

He went over and got into the Miata. Connor gave the horn a derisive beep and drove off down the lane without a backward glance, although Jerry did look back and his face was troubled.

"Aunt Alice," Andi said softly, "are you okay?"

"I will be once I take my medication," Aunt Alice said, gratefully reaching for the pill that Bruce held out to her. Andi supported her head, and she gulped it down without water and then lay back on the grass.

"I don't think any bones are broken," she said. "But I may have done something to my shoulder. I think I'll just lie here and rest until the police arrive. I have a very nice view of the sky. It's so beautifully blue and clear out here in the country. I hope the dogs have enjoyed it."

"The police!" Bruce cried. "We need to get the cell phone and call them!"

"I already did," Andi said. "While Aunt Alice kept Connor and Jerry occupied, I called nine-one-one. The police should be here any time now. I gave them a description of Connor's car, and they're going to intercept him. Then they're going to come and get us and the dogs. I'm just worried that Connor will give them that story about their getting a phone call and Aunt Alice tripping over her own feet. He was right when he bragged that he and Jerry are convincing. And there isn't any evidence to prove that they're liars."

"You're wrong about that," Bruce said. "I got pictures of everything."

He clicked on the screen of his camera to display the images. First came the one he'd taken earlier of two figures in black T-shirts, grabbing Lola off the beach towel. Then came photos of Connor's Miata parked in front of the barn; of the chicken pen jammed with dogs; of Jerry, in black shirt and baseball cap, holding the sack of dog food and grinning maliciously; of Connor, dragging Andi out of Aunt Alice's car; of Connor, jerking the purse from Aunt Alice with one hand, while shoving her hard with the other; and a final incredible action shot of Aunt Alice tumbling backward, halfway to the ground.

"Oh, my, that is a good picture, Bruce!" Aunt Alice exclaimed in admiration. "You truly do have the makings of a photojournalist. Now, I think you should go and talk to your dog. Tell him he's going to get to ride home in a police car. There aren't many dogs who can brag to their friends about *that*!"

CHAPTER EIGHTEEN

BOBBY STRIKES BACK

By Andrea Walker
THE FINAL CHAPTER

It was getting far too crowded in Mr. Rinkle's tool-shed. Dognapping had become Mr. Rinkle's hobby. He dognapped for no reason except that he would see a dog in a yard with nobody keeping an eye on it, and he would swoop in and take it.

He didn't ask for ransom. He wasn't in it for the money, he was in it for the power.

Because Andi knew how she wanted the story to turn out, she had jumped ahead to write that ending, leaving lots of empty pages between the first and final chapters. She had the rest of the summer to fill them with details, and then she planned to enter the manuscript in a contest. She had seen a poster in the library about a contest for "books by young authors" and the winner would have her book published. Andi intended to be that winner.

She had thought that it might be hard to find words for the ending, but surprisingly it wasn't. They flowed onto the paper as if they had a will of their own.

Bobby the Basset knew they had to get out. Mr. Rinkle was feeding them, but he wasn't giving them love. And the dogs didn't like being stuffed into a tiny shed that already had a lawn mower in it. Bobby wondered why neighbors weren't complaining about Mr. Rinkle's grass, since he couldn't get the mower out from under the dogs.

"I will get us all out," Bobby promised his companions. "But you will need to do exactly what I tell you, because I have the Blue Sense. All bassets have the Blue Sense. It's what makes us good hunters."

The other dogs didn't like that much, because young dogs don't like old dogs to boss them around.

But they did what Bobby said, because nobody else was doing anything, and they knew that they had to get out before they got squashed to death.

Bobby said, "Everybody climb on top of each other to make a big pile that goes to the ceiling. I will be the dog on the top of the pile."

So they stacked themselves up and made a pyramid, and Bobby was up at the top, even though he couldn't climb there by himself and the other dogs had to boost him.

"Empty your lungs," Bobby told them. "Then, when I count to three, take the deepest breath you've ever taken."

The dogs obediently let out their breaths while Bobby counted. Then, on the count of three, they all took big breaths. Their chests pushed out, and they swelled up like balloons. Bobby was pushed so hard against the ceiling that he burst right through.

Bobby the Basset stepped out onto what was left of the toolshed roof, and he felt the evening breeze, and he smelled good smells that he hadn't smelled for so long that he had forgotten what they smelled like. He raised his head and looked up at the dark night sky. In the middle of that sky there was a full white moon with a girl's face in it.

Bobby threw back his head and bayed at the moon. The girl smiled down at him.

In the morning there would be stories in the paper about dogs being found in a toolshed, and Mr. Rinkle would be arrested, and he would get lawyers to defend him, and on and on it would go until people were sick of hearing about it.

But Bobby the Basset wasn't worried about that. He just bayed at the girl in the moon and watched her smile.

Andi closed her notebook and tossed it onto her bed. This was the last night that she and Bruce would be staying with Aunt Alice. Their parents were returning in the morning, having cut their vacation short by a couple of days when they learned there was trouble at home.

Andi opened the door of her bedroom and stepped out into the hallway. At the end of the hall she could see the light from Aunt Alice's office. The door was ajar, and Andi could see her great-aunt's white head bent over the computer.

Andi walked down the hall and rapped lightly on the half-open door.

Aunt Alice looked up from the computer, and

Andi could see that she had been playing online bingo.

"Hello, dear," Aunt Alice said. "I was concerned that you might not be able to sleep, what with fretting about giving Lola to Debbie."

"I'm not sad about that," Andi said. "Debbie's always wanted a dog, and her mother wouldn't let her have one because of their cat. But the cat ran away, and Debbie's gotten bonded to Lola. She says they're two of a kind, and maybe they are. Bebe doesn't mind Lola leaving. Now she will get all my attention." She paused and then said, "I'll miss the shy, shaggy Friday I used to know. Debbie's going to keep Lola shaved because she seems to like it. I liked Lola better when she was Friday."

"Changes in life are never easy," said Aunt Alice. "But we have to go with the flow. Dogs change, people change, our views of the world keep changing — life is all about changes. Maybe Jerry will change. I certainly hope so."

"What will happen to Jerry and Connor?" Andi asked.

"I have no idea," Aunt Alice said. "Private detectives aren't involved with the legal process. We just do our job and then the authorities take over. My guess is that Mr. Gordon will pull some strings to get a plea bargain, and the whole mess will be settled out of court."

"You're not going to sue for assault and battery?" Andi asked her. Aunt Alice's shoulder had been dislocated, and she was in quite a lot of pain, although her doctors had assured her that eventually she would be fine.

"It's not worth it," Aunt Alice said. "I don't want money from the Gordons. I just want them to get counseling for their son. It would also be nice if their nephew was locked up in a juvenile facility until he turns twenty-one, but that's probably too much to hope for."

"Things don't always work out the way they ought to, do they?" Andi commented.

"No," Aunt Alice said. "But we have to keep trying to make them work right. Maybe if enough of us try, someday that will happen."

Andi thought about her novel with all those dogs stuffed into the toolshed and Bobby the Basset commanding them to work together.

"I know who I want to be when I grow up," she said.

"Of course," Aunt Alice said. "You're going to be a writer."

"I didn't say what, I said *who*," Andi said. "When I grow up I want to be *you*!"

Aunt Alice smiled. The smile wasn't just on her lips or in her eyes, it radiated out of every part of her, as if it were a light shining straight from her soul.

"Andi, dear," she said, "I know how silly this sounds, but sometimes you make me want to sing to the moon!"